THE MEN IN THE WALLS

THE MEN IN THE WALLS

by William Tenn

I

Mankind consisted of 128 people.

The sheer population pressure of so vast a horde had long ago filled over a dozen burrows. Bands of the Male Society occupied the outermost four of these interconnected corridors and patrolled it with their full strength, twenty-three young adult males in the prime of courage and alertness. They were stationed there to take the first shock of any danger to Mankind, they and their band captains and the youthful initiates who served them.

Eric the Only was an initiate in this powerful force. Today, he was a student warrior, a fetcher and a carrier for proven, seasoned men. But tomorrow, tomorrow....

This was his birthday. Tomorrow, he would be sent forth to Steal for Mankind. When he returned—and have no fear: Eric was swift, Eric was clever, he would return—off might go the loose loin cloths of boyhood to be replaced by the tight loin straps of a proud Male Society warrior.

He would be free to raise his voice and express his opinions in the Councils of Mankind. He could stare at the women whenever he liked, for as long as he liked, to approach them even—

He found himself wandering to the end of his band's burrow, still carrying the spear he was sharpening for his uncle. There, where a women's burrow began, several members of the Female Society were preparing food stolen from the Monster larder that very day. Each spell had to be performed properly, each incantation said just right, or it would not be fit to eat. It might even be dangerous. Mankind was indeed fortunate: plenty of food, readily available, and women who well understood the magical work of preparing it for human consumption.

And such women—such splendid creatures!

Sarah the Sickness-Healer, for example, with her incredible knowledge of what food was fit and what was unfit, her only garment a cloud of hair that alternately screened and revealed her hips and

5

breasts, the largest in all Mankind. There was a woman for you! Over five litters she had had, two of them of maximum size.

Eric watched as she turned a yellow chunk of food around and around under the glow lamp hanging from the ceiling of the burrow, looking for she only knew what and recognizing it when she found it she only knew how. A man could really strut with such a mate.

But she was the wife of a band leader and far, far beyond him. Her daughter, though, Selma the Soft-Skinned, would probably be flattered by his attentions. She still wore her hair in a heavy bun: it would be at least a year before the Female Society would consider her an initiate and allow her to drape it about her nakedness. No, far too young and unimportant for a man on the very verge of warrior status.

Another girl caught his eye. She had been observing him for some time and smiling behind her lashes, behind her demurely set mouth. Harriet the History-Teller, the oldest daughter of Rita the Record-Keeper, who would one day succeed to her mother's office. Now there was a lovely, slender girl, her hair completely unwound in testament to full womanhood and recognized professional status.

*   *   *   *   *

Eric had caught these covert, barely stated smiles from her before; especially in the last few weeks, as the time for his Theft approached. He knew that if he were successful—and he *had* to be successful: don't dare think of anything but success!—she would look with favor on advances from him. Of course, Harriet was a redhead, and therefore, according to Mankind's traditions, unlucky. She was probably having a hard time finding a mate. But his own mother had been a redhead.

Yes, and his mother had been very unlucky indeed.

Even his father had been infected with her terrible bad luck. Still, Harriet the History-Teller was an important person in the tribe for one her age. Good-looking too. And, above all, she didn't turn away from him. She smiled at him, openly now. He smiled back.

"Look at Eric!" he heard someone call out behind him. "He's already searching for a mate. Hey, Eric! You've not even wearing straps yet. First comes the stealing. *Then* comes the mating."

Eric spun around, bits of fantasy still stuck to his lips.

The group of young men lounging against the wall of his band's burrow were tossing laughter back and forth between them. They were all adults: they had all made their Theft. Socially, they were still his superiors. His only recourse was cold dignity.

"I know that," he began. "There is no mating until—"

"Until never for some people," one of the young men broke in. He rattled his spear in his hand, carelessly, proudly. "After you steal, you still have to convince a woman that you're a man. And some men have to do an awful lot of convincing. An *awful* lot, Eric-O."

The ball of laughter bounced back and forth again, heavier than before. Eric the Only felt his face turn bright red. How dare they remind him of his birth? On this day of all days? Here he was about to prepare himself to go forth and Steal for Mankind....

He dropped the sharpening stone into his pouch and slid his right hand back along his uncle's spear. "At least," he said, slowly and definitely, "at least, my woman will stay convinced, Roy the Runner. She won't be always open to offers from every other man in the tribe."

"You lousy little throwback!" Roy the Runner yelled. He leaped away from the rest of the band and into a crouch facing Eric, his spear tense in one hand. "You're asking for a hole in the belly! My woman's had two litters off me, two big litters. What would you have given her, you dirty singleton?"

"She's had two litters, but not off you," Eric the Only spat, holding his spear out in the guard position. "If you're the father, then the chief's blonde hair is contagious—like measles."

Roy bellowed and jabbed his spear forward. Eric parried it and lunged in his turn. He missed as his opponent leaped to one side. They circled each other, cursing and insulting, eyes only for the point of each other's spears. The other young men had scrambled a distance down the burrow to get out of their way.

*   *   *   *   *

A powerful arm suddenly clamped Eric's waist from behind and lifted him off his feet. He was kicked hard, so that he stumbled a half-dozen steps and fell. On his feet in a moment, the spear still in his hand, he whirled, ready to deal with this new opponent. He was mad enough to fight all Mankind.

But not Thomas the Trap-Smasher. No, not that mad.

All the tension drained out of him as he recognized the captain of his band. He couldn't fight Thomas. His uncle. And the greatest of all men. Guiltily, he walked to the niche in the wall where the band's weapons were stacked and slid his uncle's spear into its appointed place.

"What the hell's the matter with you, Roy?" Thomas was asking behind him. "Fighting a duel with an initiate? Where's your band spirit? That's all we need these days, to be cut down from six effectives to five. Save your spear for Strangers, or—if you feel very brave—for Monsters. But don't show a point in our band's burrow if you know what's good for you, hear me?"

"I wasn't fighting a duel," the Runner mumbled, sheathing his own spear. "The kid got above himself. I was punishing him."

"You punish with the haft of the spear. And anyway, this is my band and I do the punishing around here. Now move on out, all of you, and get ready for the council. I'll attend to the boy myself."

They went off obediently without looking back. The Trap-Smasher's band was famous for its discipline throughout the length and breadth of Mankind. A proud thing to be a member of it. But to be called a boy in front of the others! A boy, when he was full-grown and ready to begin stealing!

Although, come to think of it, he'd rather be called a boy than a singleton. A boy eventually became a man, but a singleton stayed a singleton forever. He put the problem to his uncle who was at the niche, inspecting the band's reserve pile of spears.

"Isn't it possible—I mean, it is possible, isn't it—that my father had some children by another woman? You told me he was one of the best thieves we ever had."

The captain of the band turned to study him, folding his arms across his chest so that biceps swelled into greatness and power. They glinted in the light of the tiny lantern bound to his forehead, the glow lantern that only fully accredited warriors might wear. After a while, the older man shook his head and said, very gently:

"Eric, Eric, forget about it, boy. He was all of those things and more. Your father was famous. Eric the Storeroom-Stormer, we called him, Eric the Laugher at Locks, Eric the Roistering Robber of all Mankind. He taught me everything I know. But he only married once. And if any other woman ever played around with him, she's been careful to keep it a secret. Now dress up those spears. You've let them get all sloppy. Butts together, that's the way, points up and even with each other."

*   *   *   *   *

Dutifully, Eric rearranged the bundle of armament that was his responsibility. He turned to his uncle again, now examining the knapsacks and canteens that would be carried on the expedition. "Suppose there had been another woman. My father could have had two, three, even four litters by different women. Extra-large litters too. If we could prove something like that, I wouldn't be a singleton any more. I would not be Eric the Only."

The Trap-Smasher sighed and thought for a moment. Then he pulled the spear from his back sling and took Eric's arm. He drew the youth along the burrow until they stood alone in the very center of it. He looked carefully at the exits at either end, making certain that they were completely alone before giving his reply in an unusually low, guarded voice.

THE MEN IN THE WALLS

"We'd never be able to prove anything like that. If you don't want to be Eric the Only, if you want to be Eric the something-else, well then, it's up to you. You have to make a good Theft. That's what you should be thinking about all the time now—your Theft. Eric, which category are you going to announce?"

He hadn't thought about it very much. "The usual one I guess. The one that's picked for most initiations. First category."

The older man brought his lips together, looking dissatisfied. "First category. *Food.* Well...."

Eric felt he understood. "You mean, for someone like me—an Only, who's really got to make a name for himself—I ought to announce like a real warrior? I should say I'm going to steal in the second category—Articles Useful to Mankind. Is that what my father would have done?"

"Do you know what your father would have done?"

"No. What?" Eric demanded eagerly.

"He'd have elected the third category. That's what I'd be announcing these days, if I were going through an initiation ceremony. That's what I want you to announce."

"Third category? Monster souvenirs? But no one's elected the third category in I don't know how many auld lang synes. Why should I do it?"

"Because this is more than just an initiation ceremony. It could be the beginning of a new life for all of us."

Eric frowned. What could be more than an initiation ceremony and his attainment of full thieving manhood?

"There are things going on in Mankind, these days," Thomas the Trap-Smasher continued in a strange, urgent voice. "Big things. And you're going to be a part of them. This Theft of yours—if you handle it right, if you do what I tell you, it's likely to blow the lid off everything the chief has been sitting on."

10

"The *chief?*" Eric felt confused. He was walking up a strange burrow now without a glow lamp. "What's the chief got to do with my Theft?"

*   *   *   *   *

His uncle examined both ends of the corridor again. "Eric, what's the most important thing we, or you, or anyone, can do? What is our life all about? What are we here for?"

"That's easy," Eric chuckled. "That's the easiest question there is. A child could answer it:

"*Hit back at the Monsters,*" he quoted. "*Drive them from the planet, if we can. Regain Earth for Mankind, if we can. But above all, hit back at the Monsters. Make them suffer as they've made us suffer. Make them know we're still here, we're still fighting. Hit back at the Monsters.*"

"Hit back at the Monsters. Right. Now how have we been doing that?"

Eric the Only stared at his uncle. That wasn't the next question in the catechism. He must have heard incorrectly. His uncle couldn't have made a mistake in such a basic ritual.

"*We will do that,*" he went on in the second reply, his voice sliding into the singsong of childhood lessons, "*by regaining the science and knowhow of our fore-fathers. Man was once Lord of all Creation: his science and knowhow made him supreme. Science and knowhow is what we need to hit back at the Monsters.*"

"Now, Eric," his uncle asked gently. "Please tell me this. What in hell is knowhow?"

That was way off. They were a full corridor's length from the normal progression of the catechism now.

"Knowhow is—knowhow is—" he stumbled over the unfamiliar verbal terrain. "Well, it's what our ancestors knew. And what they did with it, I guess. Knowhow is what you need before you can make hydrogen bombs or economic warfare or guided missiles, any of those really big weapons like our ancestors had."

THE MEN IN THE WALLS

"Did those weapons do them any good? Against the Monsters, I mean. Did they stop the Monsters?"

Eric looked completely blank for a moment, then brightened. Oh! He knew the way now. He knew how to get back to the catechism:

"*The suddenness of the attack, the—*"

"Stop it!" his uncle ordered. "Don't give me any of that garbage! *The suddenness of the attack, the treachery of the Monsters*—does it sound like an explanation to you? Honestly? If our ancestors were really Lords of Creation and had such great weapons, would the Monsters have been able to conquer them? I've led my band on dozens of raids, and I know the value of a surprise attack; but believe me, boy, it's only good for a flash charge and a quick getaway if you're facing a superior force. You can knock somebody down when he doesn't expect it. But if he really has more than you, he won't *stay* down. Right?"

"I—I guess so. I wouldn't know."

"Well, I know. I know from plenty of battle experience. The thing to remember is that once our ancestors were knocked down, they stayed down. That means their science and knowhow were not so much in the first place. And *that* means—" here he turned his head and looked directly into Eric's eyes—" *that* means the science of our ancestors wasn't worth one good damn against the Monsters, and it wouldn't be worth one good damn to us!"

Eric the Only turned pale. He knew heresy when he heard it.

* * * * *

His uncle patted him on the shoulder, drawing a deep breath as if he'd finally spat out something extremely unpleasant. He leaned closer, eyes glittering beneath the forehead glow lamp and his voice dropped to a fierce whisper.

"Eric. When I asked you how we've been hitting back at the Monsters, you told me what we *ought* to do. We haven't been *doing* a single thing to bother them. We don't know how to reconstruct the Ancestor-science, we don't have the tools or weapons or knowhow—whatever *that* is—but they wouldn't do us a bit of good even if we had them. Because they failed once. They failed completely and at their best. There's just no point in trying to put them together again."

And now Eric understood. He understood why his uncle had whispered, why there had been so much strain in this conversation. Bloodshed was involved here, bloodshed and death.

"Uncle Thomas," he whispered, in a voice that kept cracking despite his efforts to keep it whole and steady, "how long have you been an Alien-Science man? When did you leave Ancestor-Science?"

Thomas the Trap-Smasher caressed his spear before he answered. He felt for it with a gentle, wandering arm, almost unconsciously, but both of them registered the fact that it was loose and ready. His tremendous body, nude except for the straps about his loins and the light spear-sling on his back, looked as if it were preparing to move instantaneously in any direction.

He stared again from one end of the burrow to the other, his forehead lamp reaching out to the branching darkness of the exits. Eric stared with him. No one was leaning tightly against a wall and listening.

"How long? Since I got to know your father. He was in another band; naturally we hadn't seen much of each other before he married my sister. I'd heard about him, though: everyone in the Male Society had—he was a great thief. But once he became my brother-in-law, I learned a lot from him. I learned about locks, about the latest traps—and I learned about Alien-Science. He'd been an Alien-Science man for years. He converted your mother, and he converted me."

Eric the Only backed away. "No!" he called out wildly. "Not my father and mother! They were decent people—when they were killed a service was held in their name—they went to add to the science of our ancestors—"

    *   *   *   *   *

THE MEN IN THE WALLS

His uncle jammed a powerful hand over his mouth.

"Shut up, you damn fool, or you'll finish us both! Of course your parents were decent people. How do you think they were killed? Your mother was with your father out in Monster territory. Have you ever heard of a woman going along with her husband on a Theft? And taking her baby with her? Do you think it was an ordinary robbery of the Monsters? They were Alien-science people, serving their faith as best they could. They died for it."

Eric looked into his uncle's eyes over the hand that covered the lower half of his face. *Alien-science people ... serving their faith ... do you think it was an ordinary robbery ... they died for it!*

He had never realized before how odd it was that his parents had gone to Monster territory together, a man taking his wife and the woman taking her baby!

As he relaxed, his uncle removed the gagging hand. "What kind of Theft was it that my parents died in?"

Thomas examined his face and seemed satisfied. "The kind you're going after," he said. "If you are your father's son. If you're man enough to continue the work he started. Are you?"

Eric started to nod, then found himself shrugging weakly, and finally just hung his head. He didn't know what to say. His uncle—well, his uncle was his model and his leader, and he was strong and wise and crafty. His father—naturally, he wanted to emulate his father and continue whatever work he had started. But this was his initiation ceremony, after all, and there would be enough danger merely in proving his manhood. For his initiation ceremony to take on a task that had destroyed his father, the greatest thief the tribe had ever known, and a heretical, blasphemous task at that....

"I'll try. I don't know if I can."

"You can," his uncle told him heartily. "It's been set up for you. It will be like walking through a dug burrow, Eric. All you have to face through is the council. You'll have to be steady there, no matter what. You tell the chief that you're undertaking the third category."

WILLIAM TENN

"But why the third?" Eric asked. "Why does it have to be Monster souvenirs?"

"Because that's what we need. And you stick to it, no matter what pressure they put on you. Remember, an initiate has the right to decide what he's going to steal. A man's first Theft is his own affair."

"But, listen, uncle—"

There was a whistle from the end of the burrow. Thomas the Trap-Smasher nodded in the direction of the signal.

"The council's beginning, boy. We'll talk later, on expedition. Now remember this: stealing from the third category is your own idea, and all your own idea. Forget everything else we've talked about. If you hit any trouble with the chief, I'll be there. I'm your sponsor, after all."

He threw an arm about his confused nephew and walked to the end of the burrow where the other members of the band waited.

II

The tribe had gathered in its central and largest burrow under the great, hanging glow lamps that might be used in this place alone. Except for the few sentinels on duty in the outlying corridors, all of Mankind was here. It was an awesome sight to behold.

On the little hillock known as the Royal Mound, lolled Franklin the Father of Many Thieves, Chieftain of all Mankind. He alone of the cluster of warriors displayed heaviness of belly and flabbiness of arm—for he alone had the privilege of a sedentary life. Beside the sternly muscled band leaders who formed his immediate background, he looked almost womanly; and yet one of his many titles was simply The Man.

Yes, unquestionably The Man of Mankind was Franklin the Father of Many Thieves. You could tell it from the hushed, respectful attitudes of the subordinate warriors who stood at a distance from the mound. You could tell it from the rippling interest of the women as they stood on the other side of the great burrow, drawn up in the ranks of the Female Society. You could tell it from the nervousness and scorn with which the women were watched by their leader, Ottilie, the Chieftain's First Wife. And finally, you could tell it from the faces of the children, standing in a distant, disorganized bunch. A clear majority of their faces bore an unmistakable resemblance to Franklin's.

Franklin clapped his hands, three evenly spaced, flesh-heavy wallops.

"In the name of our ancestors," he said, "and the science with which they ruled the Earth, I declare this council opened. May it end as one more step in the regaining of their science. Who asked for a council?"

"I did." Thomas the Trap-Smasher moved out of his band and stood before the chief.

Franklin nodded, and went on with the next, formal question:

"And your reason?"

"As a band leader, I call attention to a candidate for manhood. A member of my band, a spear-carrier for the required time, and an accepted apprentice in the Male Society. My nephew, Eric the Only."

As his name was sung out, Eric shook himself. Half on his own volition and half in response to the pushes he received from the other warriors, he stumbled up to his uncle and faced the chief. This, the most important moment of his life, was proving almost too much for him. So many people in one place, accredited and famous warriors, knowledgeable and attractive women, the chief himself, all this after the shattering revelations from his uncle—he was finding it hard to think clearly. And it was vital to think clearly. His responses to the next few questions had to be exactly right.

*   *   *   *   *

The chief was asking the first: "Eric the Only, do you apply for full manhood?"

Eric breathed hard and nodded. "I do."

16

"As a full man, what will be your value to Mankind?"

"I will steal for Mankind whatever it needs. I will defend Mankind against all outsiders. I will increase the possessions and knowledge of the Female Society so that the Female Society can increase the power and well-being of Mankind."

"And all this you swear to do?"

"And all this I swear to do."

The Chief turned to Eric's uncle. "As his sponsor, do you support his oath and swear that he is to be trusted?"

With just the faintest hint of sarcasm in his voice, Thomas the Trap-Smasher replied: "Yes. I support his oath and swear that he is to be trusted."

There was a rattling moment, the barest second, when the chief's eyes locked with those of the band leader. With all that was on Eric's mind at the moment, he noticed it. Then the chief looked away and pointed to the women on the other side of the burrow.

"He is accepted as a candidate by the men. Now the women must ask for proof, for only a woman's proof bestows full manhood."

The first part was over. And it hadn't been too bad. Eric turned to face the advancing leaders of the Female Society, Ottilie, the Chieftain's First Wife, in the center. Now came the part that scared him. The women's part.

As was customary at such a moment, his uncle and sponsor left him when the women came forward. Thomas the Trap-Smasher led his band to the warriors grouped about the Throne Mound. There, with their colleagues, they folded their arms across their chests and turned to watch. A man can only give proof of his manhood while he is alone; his friends cannot support him once the women approach.

It was not going to be easy, Eric realized. He had hoped that at least one of his uncle's wives would be among the three examiners: they were both kindly people who liked him and had talked to him much about the mysteries of women's work. But he had drawn a trio of hard-faced females who apparently intended to take him over the full course before they passed him.

Sarah the Sickness-Healer opened the proceedings. She circled him belligerently, hands on hips, her great breasts rolling to and fro like a pair of swollen pendulums, her eyes glittering with scorn.

"Eric the Only," she intoned, and then paused to grin, as if it were a name impossible to believe, "Eric the Singleton, Eric the one and only child of either his mother or his father. Your parents almost didn't have enough between them to make a solitary child. Is there enough in you to make a man?"

*　　*　　*　　*　　*

There was a snigger of appreciation from the children in the distance, and it was echoed by a few growling laughs from the vicinity of the Throne Mound. Eric felt his face and neck go red. He would have fought any man to the death for remarks like these. Any man at all. But who could lift his hand to a woman and be allowed to live? Besides, one of the main purposes of this exhibition was to investigate his powers of self-control.

"I think so," he managed to say after a long pause. "And I'm willing to prove it."

"Prove it, then!" the woman snarled. Her right hand, holding a long, sharp-pointed pin, shot to his chest like a flung spear. Eric made his muscles rigid and tried to send his mind away. That, the men had told him, was what you had to do at this moment: it was not you they were hurting, not you at all. You, your mind, your knowledge of self, were in another part of the burrow entirely, watching these painful things being done to someone else.

The pin sank into his chest for a little distance, paused, came out. It probed here, probed there; finally it found a nerve in his upper arm. There, guided by the knowledge of the Sickness-Healer, it bit and clawed at the delicate area until Eric felt he would grind his teeth to powder in the effort not to cry out. His clenched fists twisted agonizingly at the ends of his arms in a paroxysm of protest, but he kept his body still. He didn't cry out; he didn't move away; he didn't raise a hand to protect himself.

Sarah the Sickness-Healer stepped back and considered him. "There is no man here yet," she said grudgingly. "But perhaps there is the beginnings of one."

He could relax. The physical test was over. There would be another one, much later, after he had completed his theft successfully; but that would be exclusively by men as part of his proud initiation ceremony. Under the circumstances, he knew he would be able to go through it almost gaily.

Meanwhile, the women's physical test was over. That was the important thing for now. In sheer reaction, his body gushed forth sweat which slid over the bloody cracks in his skin and stung viciously. He felt the water pouring down his back and forced himself not to go limp, prodded his mind into alertness.

"Did that hurt?" he was being asked by Rita, the old crone of a Record-Keeper. There was a solicitous smile on her forty-year-old face, but he knew it was a fake. A woman as old as that no longer felt sorry for anybody. She had too many aches and pains and things generally wrong with her to worry about other people's troubles.

"A little," he said. "Not much."

"The Monsters will hurt you much more if they catch you stealing from them, do you know that? They will hurt you much more than we ever could."

"I know. But the stealing is more important than the risk I'm taking. The stealing is the most important thing a man can do."

* * * * *

Rita the Record-Keeper nodded. "Because you steal things Mankind needs in order to live. You steal things that the Female Society can make into food, clothing and weapons for Mankind, so that Mankind can live and flourish."

19

THE MEN IN THE WALLS

He saw the way, saw what was expected of him. "No," he contradicted her. "That's not why we steal. We live on what we steal, but we do not steal just to go on living."

"Why?" she asked blandly, as if she didn't know the answer better than any other member of the tribe. "Why do we steal? What is more important than survival?"

Here it was now. The catechism.

"To hit back at the Monsters," he began. *"To drive them from the planet, if we can. Regain Earth for Mankind, if we can. But, above all, hit back at the Monsters...."*

He ploughed through the long verbal ritual, pausing at the end of each part, so that the Record-Keeper could ask the proper question and initiate the next sequence.

She tried to trip him once. She reversed the order of the fifth and sixth questions. Instead of *"What will we do with the Monsters when we have regained the Earth from them?"* she asked, *"Why can't we use the Monsters' own Alien-Science to fight the Monsters?"*

Carried along by mental habit, Eric was well into the passage beginning *"We will keep them as our ancestors kept all strange animals, in a place called a zoo, or we will drive them into our burrows and force them to live as we have lived,"* before he realized the switch and stopped in confusion. Then he got a grip on himself, sought the right answer in his memory with calmness, as his uncle's wives had schooled him to do, and began again.

"There are three reasons why we cannot ever use Alien-Science," he recited, holding up his hand with the thumb and little finger closed. *"Alien-Science is non-human, Alien-Science is inhuman, Alien-Science is anti-human. First, since it is non-human,"* he closed his forefinger, *"we cannot use it because we can never understand it. And because it is inhuman, we would never want to use it even if we could understand it. And because it is anti-human and can only be used to hurt and damage Mankind, we would not be able to use it so long as we remain human ourselves. Alien-Science is the opposite of Ancestor-Science in every way,*

ugly instead of beautiful, hurtful instead of helpful. When we die, Alien-Science would not bring us to the world of our ancestors, but to another world full of Monsters."

*   *   *   *   *

All in all, it went very well, despite the trap into which he had almost fallen.

But he couldn't help remembering the conversation with his uncle in the other burrow. As his mouth reeled off the familiar words and concepts, his mind kept wondering how the two fitted together. His uncle was Alien-Science, and, according to his uncle, so had been his parents. Did that make them non-human, inhuman, anti-human?

And what did it make him? He knew his religious duty well: he should at this moment be telling all Mankind about his uncle's horrible secret.

The whole subject was far too complicated for someone with his limited experience.

When he had completed the lengthy catechism, Rita the Record-Keeper said: "And this is what you say about the science of our ancestors. Now we will find out what the science of our ancestors says about you."

She signaled over her shoulder, without turning her head, and two young girls—female apprentices—pulled forward the large record machine which was the very center of the tribe's religious life. They stepped back, both smiling shyly and encouragingly at Eric the Only.

He knew the smiles meant little more than simple best wishes from apprentices of one sex to apprentices of the other, but even that was quite a bit at the moment. It meant that he was much closer to full status than they. It meant that, in the opinion of unprejudiced, disinterested observers, his examination was proceeding very well indeed.

Singleton, he thought fiercely to himself. *I'll show them what a singleton can do!*

THE MEN IN THE WALLS

Rita the Record-Keeper turned a knob at the top of the squat machine and it began to hum. She flung her arms up, quiveringly apart, and all, warriors, women, children, apprentices, even the chief himself, all bowed their heads.

"Harken to the words of our ancestors," she chanted. "Watch closely the spectacle of their great achievements. When their end was upon them, and they knew that only we, their descendants, might regain the Earth they had lost, they made this machine for the future generations of Mankind as a guide to the science that once had been and must be again."

The old woman lowered her arms. Simultaneously, heads went up all over the burrow and stared expectantly at the wall opposite the record machine, waiting for the magic message.

"Eric the Only," Rita called, spinning the dial on the left of the machine with one hand and stabbing at it randomly with the forefinger of the other. "This is the sequence in the science of our ancestors that speaks for you alone. This is the appointed vision under which you will live and die."

*   *   *   *   *

He stared at the wall, breathing hard. Now he would find out what his life was to be about—*now*! His uncle's vision at this moment, years ago, had suggested the nickname he came to bear: the Trap-Smasher. At the last initiation ceremony, a youth had called forth a sequence in which two enormous airborne vehicles of the ancestors had collided.

They'd tried to cheer the boy up, but he'd known his fate was upon him. Sure enough, he had been caught by a monster in the middle of his Theft and dashed to pieces against a wall.

Even then, Eric decided, he'd rather have that kind of a sequence than the awful emptiness of a *blank* vision. When, every once in a while, the machine went on and showed nothing but a blinding white rectangle, the whole tribe knew that the youth being examined had no possibility of manhood in him at all. And the machine was never wrong. A boy who'd drawn a blank vision inevitably became more and more effeminate as he grew older without ever going out on his Theft. He tended to shun the company of warriors and to ask the women for minor tasks to perform. The machine of the ancestors looked at a boy and told exactly what he was and what he would become.

It had been great, that science which had produced this machine, no doubt about it. There was a power source in it which was self-contained, and which was supposed to be like the power behind all things. It would run almost forever, if the machine were not tampered with—although who could dream of tampering with it? In its visions were locked, not only the secrets of every individual human being, but enormous mysteries which the whole of Mankind had to solve before it could work out its salvation through the rituals and powers of the ancestral science.

Now, however, there was only one small part of Mankind that concerned Eric. Himself. His future. He waited, growing more and more tense as the power hum from the machine increased in pitch. And suddenly there was a grunt of awe from the entire burrow of people as a vision was thrown upon the wall.

He hadn't drawn a blank. That was the most important thing. He had been given an authentic ancestral vision.

"Scattergood's does it again!" a voice blared, as the picture projected on the wall showed people coming from all directions, wearing the strange body wrappings of the ancestors. They rushed, men, women, children, from the four corners of the glittering screen to some strange structure in the center and disappeared into its entrance. More and more poured in, more and more kept materializing at the edges and scrambling toward the structure in the center.

"Scattergood's does it again!" the vision yelled out at them. "The sale of sales! The value of values! Only at Scattergood's three stores tomorrow. Binoculars, tape recorders, cameras, all at tremendous reductions, many below cost. Value, value, value!"

Now the vision showed only objects. Strange, unfamiliar objects such as the ancestors used. And as each object appeared, the voice recited a charm over it. Powerful and ancient magic this, the forgotten lore of Ancestor-Science.

"Krafft-Yahrmann Exposure Meters, the best there is, you've heard about them and now you can buy them, the light meter that's an eye-opener, a price to fit every pocketbook, eight dollars and ninety-five cents, tomorrow at Scattergood's, absolutely only one to a customer.

"Kyoto Automatic Eight-Millimeter Movie Cameras with an f 1.4 lens and an electric eye that does all the focusing and gives you a perfect exposure every single time. As low as three dollars a week. The supply is limited, so hurry, hurry, hurry!"

*   *   *   *   *

Eric watched the sequence unfold, his hands squeezing each other, his eyes almost distended in reverence and concentration. This was the clue to his life, to what he might become. This was the sequence that the record machine of the ancestors, turned on at random, had vouchsafed as a prophecy of his future.

All knowledge was in that machine—and no possibility of error.

But Eric was getting worried. The vision was so strange. Sometimes there would be a vision that baffled even the wisest women. And that meant the youth who had called it forth would always be a puzzle, to himself and all of Mankind.

Let it not happen to him! O ancestors, O science, O record machine, let it not happen to him!

Let him only have a clear and definite vision so that his personality could be clear and definite for the rest of his life!

"Our special imported high-power precision binoculars," the voice roared on as a man appeared in the vision and brought one of the strange objects up to his eyes. "If we told you the manufacturer's name, you'd recognize it immediately. 7 x 50, only fourteen dollars and ninety-five cents, *with case*. 10 x 50, only fifteen dollars and ninety-five cents, *with case*. You see further, you see clearer, you pay less. You always pay less at Scattergood's. Rock-bottom prices! Skyscraper values! Tomorrow, tomorrow, tomorrow, at Scattergood's annual week-after-Hallowe'en Sale!"

There was a click as the vision went off abruptly to be replaced by a white rectangle on the wall of the burrow. Eric realized that this was all the clue there was to be to his life. What did it mean? Could it be interpreted?

Anxiously, now, he turned to Ottilie, the Chieftain's First Wife. He turned to her as everyone else in Mankind was now turning, Sarah the Sickness-Healer and Rita the Record-Keeper amongst them.

Only Ottilie could read a vision, only short, squat, imperious Ottilie. The Chieftain's First Wife was her title of honor and her latest title, but long before she had acquired that, long before even she had become Head of the Female Society, she had been Ottilie the Augur, Ottilie the Omen-Teller, Ottilie who could walk in her mind from the homey burrow of the present into the dark, labyrinthine corridors of the future, Ottilie who could read signs, Ottilie who could announce portents.

     *   *   *   *   *

It was as Ottilie the Augur that she could pick out the one new-born babe in a litter of three that had to be destroyed because, in some way or other, it would one day bring death to its people. It was as Ottilie the Augur that, upon the death of the old chief, she had chosen Franklin the Father of Many Thieves to take over the leadership of Mankind since he stimulated the most propitious omens. In everything she had been right. And now, once again it was as Ottilie the Augur that she threw her arms over her head and twisted and swayed and moaned as she sought deep inside herself for the meaning of Eric's vision, it was as Ottilie the Augur and not as

THE MEN IN THE WALLS

Ottilie the Chieftain's First Wife, for that she had been only since Franklin had ascended the Throne Mound.

The scratches and holes gouged in his body by Sarah the Sickness-Healer had begun to ache badly, but Eric shrugged off their annoyance. Could his vision be interpreted? And *how* would it be interpreted?

Whatever Ottilie saw in the vision would stick to him for the rest of his life, much closer than the dried blood upon his arms and legs and chest. How could you possibly interpret such a vision? Eric the Scattergood? That was meaningless. Eric the Value?

No, that was a little better, but it was dreadfully vague, almost as bad as a blank vision.

He stared past Ottilie's writhing figure to where his uncle stood, surrounded by his band, a little to the left of the Throne Mound. Thomas the Trap-Smasher was watching Ottilie and grinning with all his teeth.

What did he find so funny, Eric wondered desperately? Was there nothing holy to him? Didn't he realize how important it was to Eric's future that his vision be readable, that he get a name to be proud of? What was funny in Ottilie's agony as she gave birth to Eric's future?

He realized that Ottilie was beginning to make coherent sounds. He strained his ears to listen. This, this was it. Who he really was. Who he would be, for all his life.

"Three times," Ottilie mumbled in a voice that steadily grew clearer and louder, "three times our ancestors gave Eric his name. Three repetitions they made. Three different ways they called on him to become what their science needed him to be. And all of you heard it, and I heard it, and Eric heard it too."

Which, Eric puzzled, which among the many strange magical statements had contained his name and his life's-work? He waited for the Augur to come out with it. He had almost given up breathing.

Her body relaxed now, her hands hanging at her sides, Ottilie was speaking to them in a sharp, authoritative voice as she stared at the wall of the burrow where the vision had appeared.

"'A light meter that's an eye-opener,' the Ancestor-science said," she reminded them. "And 'an electric eye that does all the focusing.' And 'you see further, you see clearer, you pay less,' the Record-Machine told us of Eric. What the ancestors want of Eric is unmistakable, what he must be if we are to hit back at the Monsters and regain the Earth which is rightfully ours."

*   *   *   *   *

Thank the record machine, thank each and every ancestor! At least the message had been unmistakable. But what precisely had it been?

Ottilie the Augur, the Omen-Teller, turned to face him now where he stood apart from the rest of eagerly-watching Mankind. He straightened up and stood stiffly to learn his fate.

"Eric," she said. "Eric the Only, Eric the Singleton, you go out now to make your Theft. If you are successful and return alive, you will become a man. And as a man you will no longer be Eric the Only, you will be Eric the Eye. Eric the Eye, Eric the Espier, Eric who seeks out the path for Mankind. Eric who hits back at the Monsters with his eye, his open eye, his electric eye, his further-seeing, clearer-seeing, less-paying eye. For this is the word of the ancestors, and all of you have heard it."

At last Eric could take a deep breath, and he did so now, noisily, in common with the whole of Mankind who had been hanging on Ottilie's words. Eric the Eye—that was what he was to be. If he was successful ... and if he lived.

Eric the Eye. Eric the Espier. Now he knew about himself. It was fixed, and for all time. It was a good name to bear, a fine personality to have. He had been very fortunate.

Rita the Record-Keeper and her daughter Harriet the History-Teller, rolled the record machine back into its accustomed holy place, the niche in the wall behind the Throne Mound. Despite

27

the sacred quality of the act in which she was engaged, the younger woman could not take her eyes off Eric. He was a person of consequence now, or at least would be when he returned. Other young and mating-aged women, he noticed, were looking at him the same way.

He began to walk around in a little circle before Mankind, and, as he walked, he strutted. He waited until Ottilie, no longer the Augur now, no longer the Omen-Teller, but once more the Chieftain's First Wife—he waited until she had returned to her place at the head of the Female Society, before he began to sing.

He threw back his head and spread out his arms and danced proudly, stampingly, before Mankind. He spun around in great dizzying circles and leaped in the air and came down with wrenching spasmodic twists of his legs and arms. And as he danced, he sang.

He sang out of the pride that racked his chest like a soul coughing, out of the majesty of the warrior-that-was-to-be, out of his sure knowledge of self. And he sang his promise to his fellows:

I am Eric the Eye, Eric the Open Eye, Eric the Electric Eye, Eric the Further-Seeing, Clearer-Seeing, Less-Paying Eye. Eric the Espier— Eric who finds and points out the way. Are you lost in a strange place? I will show you the path to your home. Does the burrow break off in too many branches? I will pick out the best one and Mankind shall walk through in safety. Are there enemies about, hidden traps, unthought-of dangers? I will see them and give warning of them in time. I will walk at the head of the line of warriors and see for them, And they shall be confident and they shall conquer— For they have Eric the Espier to lead the way and point the path!

       *   *   *   *   *

So he sang as he danced before Mankind, under the enormous glow lamps of its great central burrow. He sang of his mission in life as just a few short auld lang synes ago he had heard Roy the Runner, at his initiation, sing of the fleetness and swiftness that he would soon be the master of; as his Uncle Thomas had sung long before that of his coming ability to detect and dismantle traps; as once his own father had sung of the robberies he was to commit, of the storerooms he would empty for the benefit of Mankind. He sang and he leaped and he whirled, and all the while the watching host of Mankind beat time with its feet and hands and played chorus in the litany of his triumph.

Then came a loud grunt from Franklin the Father of Many Thieves. The noise stopped. Eric danced to a quivering halt, his body wet all over, his limbs still trembling.

"That is what is to be," Franklin pointed out, "once the Theft has been made. But first, first comes the Theft. Always before manhood comes the Theft. Now let us speak of your Theft."

"I will go into the very home of the Monsters," Eric announced proudly, his head thrown back before the chief. "I will go into their home alone, with no companion but my own weapons, as a warrior should. I will steal from them, no matter what the danger, no matter what the threat. And what I steal, I will bring back for the use and enjoyment of Mankind."

Franklin nodded and made the formal reply. "That is good, and it is spoken like a warrior. What do you promise to steal from the Monsters? For your first Theft must be a promise made in advance and kept, kept exactly."

Now they were at it. Eric glanced at his uncle for support. Thomas the Trap-Smasher was staring off in a different direction. Eric licked his lips. Well, maybe it wouldn't be too bad. After all, a youth going off on his first Theft had complete freedom of choice.

"I promise to make my theft in the third category," he said, his voice trembling just a little.

The results were much more than he had anticipated. Franklin the Father of Many Thieves yelped sharply. He leaped off the Royal Mound and stood gaping at Eric for a while. His great belly and fat arms quivered with disbelief.

THE MEN IN THE WALLS

"The third category, did you say? The *third?*"

Eric, thoroughly frightened now, nodded.

Franklin turned to Chief Wife Ottilie. They both peered through the ranks of Mankind to where Thomas the Trap-Smasher stood in the midst of his band, seemingly unconcerned by the sensation that had just been created.

"What *is* this, Thomas?" the chief demanded, all ceremony and formality gone from his speech. "What are you trying to pull? What's this third category stuff you're up to?"

Thomas the Trap-Smasher turned a bland eye upon him. "What am *I* up to? I'm not up to a damn thing. The boy's got a right to pick his category. If he wants to steal in the third category, well, that's his business. What have I got to do with it?"

The chief stared at him for a few moments longer. Then he swung back to Eric and said shortly: "All right. You've chosen. The third category it is. Now let's get on with the feast."

                    *   *   *   *   *

Somehow it was all spoiled for Eric. The initiation feast that preceded a first Theft—how he had looked forward to it! But he was apparently involved in something going on in Mankind, something dangerous and unsavory.

The chief obviously considered him an important factor in whatever difficulty had arisen. Usually, an initiate about to depart on a Theft was the focus of all conversation as Mankind ate in its central burrow, the women squatting on one side, the men on the other, the children at the far ends where light was dim. But at this meal, the chief made only the most necessary ritual remarks to Eric. His eyes kept wandering from him to Thomas the Trap-Smasher.

Once in a while, Franklin's eyes met those of Ottilie, his favored and first wife, across the feast that had been spread the length of the burrow. He seemed to be saying something to her, although neither of them moved their lips. Then they would nod at each other and look back to Eric's uncle.

WILLIAM TENN

The rest of Mankind became aware of the strained atmosphere: there was little of the usual laughter and gaiety of an initiation feast. The Trap-Smasher's band had pulled in tightly all around him; most of them were not even bothering to eat but sat watchful and alert. Other band captains—men like Stephen the Strong-Armed and Harold the Hurler—had worried looks on their faces as if they were calculating highly complex problems.

Even the children were remarkably quiet. They served the food over which the women had said charms much earlier, then scurried to their places and ate with wide eyes aimed at their elders.

All in all, Eric was distinctly relieved when Franklin the Father of Many Thieves belched commandingly, stretched, and lay back on the floor of the burrow. In a few minutes, he was asleep, snoring loudly.

Night had officially begun.

III

At the end of the sleep period, as soon as the chief had awakened and yawned, thus proclaiming the dawn, Thomas the Trap-Smasher's band started on its trip.

Eric, still officially surnamed the Only, carried the precious loin straps of manhood in the food knapsack the women had provided for a possible journey of several days. They should return before the next sleep period, but when one went on an expedition into Monster territory anything might happen.

They stepped out in full military formation, a long, straggling single file, each man barely in sight of the warrior immediately ahead. For the first time in his military career, Eric was wearing only one set of spears—those for himself. Extra weapons for the band—as well as extra supplies—were on the back of a new apprentice, a stripling who marched a distance behind Eric, watching him with the same mixture of fright and exhilaration Eric himself had once accorded all other warriors.

THE MEN IN THE WALLS

Ahead of Eric, momentarily disappearing as the dim corridor curved and branched, was Roy the Runner, his long, loose-jointed legs purposefully treading down the mileage. And all the way in the lead of the column, Eric knew, was his uncle. Thomas the Trap-Smasher would be striding cautiously yet without any unnecessary waste of time, the large glow lamp on his forehead constantly shifting from wall to wall of the uninhabited burrow and then straight ahead, the heavy spear in each brawny hand ready for instant action, his mouth set to call the warning behind him if danger materialized.

To be a man—this was what it was like! To go on expeditions like this for the rest of one's life, glorious, adventure-charged expeditions so that Mankind might eat well and have weapons and live as Mankind should. And when you returned, triumphant, victorious, the welcoming dance of the women as they threaded their way through the tired ranks, giving you refreshment and taking from you the supplies that only they could turn into usable articles. Then, after you had eaten and drunk and rested, your own dance, the dance of the men, where you sang and acted out for the tribe all the events of this particular expedition, the dangers you had overcome, the splendid courage you had shown, the strange and mysterious sights you had seen.

The sights you had seen! As Eric the Eye, he would probably be entitled to a solo dance any time his band came across anything particularly curious. Oh, how high Eric the Eye would leap, how loudly, how proudly, how melodiously, he would sing of the wonders the expedition had encountered!

"Eric the Eye," the women would murmur. "What a fine, fine figure of a man! What a mate for some lucky woman!"

*   *   *   *   *

Harriet the History-Teller this morning, for example, before they started out. She had filled his canteen for him with fresh water as if he were already an accredited man instead of an initiate going out to face his ultimate trial. Before the eyes of all Mankind she had filled

32

it and brought it to him, her eyes down-cast and light purple blushes on the rosy skin of her face and body. She had treated him the way a wife treats a husband, and many warriors—Eric thought gleefully—many full warriors with their Thefts long behind them had observed that Eric was likely to join the ranks of the Male Society and the married men almost simultaneously.

Of course, with her unlucky red hair, her bustling, domineering mother, Harriet was not exactly the most marriageable girl in Mankind. Still, there were many full warriors who had not yet been able to persuade a woman to mate with them, who watched Franklin and his three wives with unconcealed hunger and envy. How they would envy Eric, the newest warrior of all, when he mated the same night he returned from his theft! Call him Only, then! Call him singleton, then!

They would have litter after litter, he and Harriet, large litters, ample litters, four, five, even six at a time. People would forget he'd ever been the product of a singleton birth. Other women, mates of other warriors, would wriggle to attract his attention as they now wriggled when they caught the eye of Franklin the Father of Many Thieves. He would make the litters fathered by Franklin look puny in comparison, he would prove that the best hope for Mankind's increase lay in his loins and his loins alone. And when the time came to select another chief....

"Hey, you damned day-dreaming singleton!" Roy the Runner was calling from the burrow ahead. "Will you wipe that haze out of your face and pay attention to signals? This is an expedition to Monster territory, not a stroll in the women's quarters. Stay alert, will you? The band captain's sent down a call for you."

Amid the chuckles ahead and behind him—damn it, even the new apprentice was laughing!—Eric took a firmer grip on his glow torch and sprinted for the head of the column. As he passed each man, he was asked the name of the girl he'd been thinking about and pressed for interesting details. Since he kept his mouth tightly shut, some of the warriors hypothesized out loud. They were painfully close to the truth.

His uncle wasn't much gentler with him. "Eric the *Eye!*" the Trap-Smasher growled. "Eric the Eyebrow, Eric the Closed Eyelash, you'll be known as, if you don't wake up! Now stay abreast of me and try to *act* like Eric the Eye. These are dangerous burrows and my vision isn't as sharp as yours. Besides, I have to fill you in on a couple of things." He turned. "Spread out a little farther back there," he called out to the men behind him. "Spread out! You should be a full spear-cast from the backside of the man in front of you. Let me see a real strung-out column with plenty of distance between each warrior."

*   *   *   *   *

To Eric, he muttered, once the maneuver had been completed: "Good. Gives us a chance to talk without everyone in the band hearing us. You can trust my bunch, but still, why take chances?"

Eric nodded, with no idea what he was talking about. His uncle had become slightly odd recently. Well, he was still the best band captain in all Mankind.

They marched along together, the light from the strange glowing substance on Eric's torch and his uncle's forehead spreading a yellowish illumination some hundred feet ahead of them. On either side, underfoot, overhead, were the curved, featureless walls of the burrow. From the center of the corridor, where they marched, the walls looked soft and spongy, but Eric knew what tremendous labor was involved in digging a niche or recess in them. It took several strong men at least two sleep periods to make a niche large enough to hold a handful of Mankind's store of artifacts.

Where had the burrows come from? Some said they had been dug by the ancestors when they had first begun to hit back at the Monsters. Others claimed the burrows had always been there, waiting for Mankind to find them and be comfortable in them.

WILLIAM TENN

In all directions the burrows stretched. On and on they went, interminably curving and branching and forking, dark and silent, until human beings stamped into them with glow lamp and glow torch. These particular corridors, Eric knew, led to Monster territory. He had been along them many times as a humble spear carrier when his uncle's band had been dispatched to bring back the necessities of life for Mankind. Other corridors went off to more exotic and even more dangerous places. But were there any places which had no burrows?

What a thought! Even the Monsters lived in burrows, big as they were reputed to be. But there was a legend that Mankind had once lived outside burrows, outside the branching corridors. Then what had they lived in? Just trying to work it out made you dizzy.

They came to a place where the burrow became two burrows, each curving away from the other in opposite directions.

"Which one?" his uncle demanded.

Eric unhesitatingly pointed the right.

Thomas the Trap-Smasher nodded. "You have a good memory," he said as he bore in the direction that Eric had indicated. "That's half of being an Eye. The other half is having a feeling, a knack, for the right way to go. You have that too. I've noticed it on every expedition where you've been along. That's what I told those women—Rita, Ottilie—I told them what your name had to be. Eric the Eye, I told them. Find a vision for the kind that corresponds to it."

*   *   *   *   *

He was so shocked that he almost came to a halt. "You picked my name? You told them what kind of vision.... That's—that's—I never heard of such a thing!"

His uncle laughed. "It's no different from Ottilie the Omen-Teller making a deal with Franklin to have a vision showing him as the new chief. He gets to be chief, she becomes the Chieftain's First Wife and automatically takes over the Female Society. Religion and politics, they're always mixed up together these days, Eric. We're not living in the old times any more when Ancestor-science was real and holy and it worked."

"It still works, Ancestor-science, doesn't it?" he pleaded. "Some of the time?"

"Everything works *some* of the time. Only Alien-science, though, works *all* of the time. It's working for Aliens, for the Monsters. It's got to begin working for us. That's where you come in."

He had to remember that his uncle was an experienced captain, a knowledgeable warrior. Thomas the Trap-Smasher's protection and advice had brought him, a despised singleton, an orphaned child of parents that no one dared even talk about, to his present estate of almost full thieving status. It was very fortunate for him that neither of his uncle's wives had yet produced a son which survived into the initiate years. He still had a lot to learn from this man.

"Now," the Trap-Smasher was saying, his eyes still on the dimly illuminated corridors ahead. "When we get to the Monster burrows, you go in. You go in alone, of course."

Well, of course, Eric thought. What other way was there to make your Theft? The first time you stole for Mankind, you did it all alone, to prove your manhood, your courage, also the amount of personal luck you enjoyed. It was not like a regular band theft—or organized stealing of a large amount of goods that would last Mankind many sleep-periods, almost a tenth of an auld lang syne. In a regular band theft, assigned to each band in rotation, a warrior had to be assured of the luck and skill of the warriors at his side. He had to know that each one of them had made his Theft—and proved himself when completely alone.

Stealing from the Monsters was dangerous enough under the best of conditions. You wanted only the cleverest, bravest, most fortunate warriors along with you.

"Once you're inside, stay close to the wall. Don't look up at first or you're likely to freeze right where you are. Keep your eyes on the wall and move close to it. Move fast."

Nothing new here. Every initiate learned over and over again, before he made his Theft, that it was terribly dangerous to look up when you first entered Monster territory. You had to keep your eyes on the wall and move in the protection of it, the wall touching your shoulder as you ran alongside it. Why this was so, Eric had no idea, but that it was so he had long ago learned to repeat as a fact.

"All right," Thomas the Trap-Smasher went on. "You turn right as you go in. *Right*, do you hear me, Eric? You turn right, without looking up, and run along the wall, letting it brush your shoulder every couple of steps. You run forty, fifty paces, and you come to a great big thing, a structure, that's almost touching the wall. You turn left along that, moving away from the wall, but still not looking up, until you pass an entrance in the structure. You don't go in that first entrance, Eric; you pass it by. About twenty, twenty-five paces further on, there'll be a second entrance, a bigger one. You go in that one."

"I go in that one," Eric repeated carefully, memorizing his uncle's words. He was receiving directions for his Theft, the most important act of his life! Every single thing his uncle told him must be listened to carefully, must not be forgotten.

"You'll be in something that looks like a burrow again, but it'll be darker, at first. The walls will soak up light from your glow lamp. After a while, the burrow will open out into a great big space, a real big and real dark space. You go on in a straight line, looking over your shoulder at the light from the entrance and making sure it's always directly behind you. You'll hit another burrow, a low one this time. Turn right at the first fork as soon as you go in, and there you are."

"Where? Where will I be? What happens then?" Eric demanded eagerly. "How do I make my Theft? Where do I find the third category?"

THE MEN IN THE WALLS

Thomas the Trap-Smasher seemed to have trouble continuing. Incredible—he was actually nervous! "There'll be a Stranger there. You tell him who you are, your name. He'll do the rest."

    *   *   *   *   *

This time Eric came to a full stop. "A Stranger?" he asked in complete amazement. "Someone who's not of Mankind?"

His uncle grabbed at his arm and pulled him along. "Well, you've seen Strangers before," he said with a weak laugh. "You know there are others in the burrows besides Mankind. You know that, don't you, boy?"

Eric certainly did.

From an early age he had accompanied his uncle and his uncle's band on warfare and trading expeditions to the burrows a bit further back. He knew that the people in these burrows looked down on the people in his, that they were more plentiful than his people, and led richer, safer lives—but he still couldn't help feeling sorry for them.

They were nothing but Strangers, after all. He was a member of Mankind.

It wasn't just that Mankind lived in the front burrows, those closest to the Monster larder. This enormous convenience might be counterbalanced, he would readily admit, by the dangers associated with it—although the constant exposure to dangers and death in every form were part of Mankind's greatness. They were great despite their inferior technology. So what if they were primarily a source of raw materials to the more populous but less hardy burrows in the rear? How long would the weaponsmiths, the potters and tanners and artificers of these burrows be able to go on with their buzzing, noisy industries once Mankind ceased to bring them the basic substances—food, cloth, metal—it had so gloriously stolen from fear-filled Monster territory? No, Mankind was the bravest, greatest, most important people in all the burrows.

But that still wasn't the point of it all.

The point was that you had nothing more to do with Strangers than was absolutely necessary. They were Strangers. You were Mankind. You stayed proudly aloof from them at all times.

Trading with them—well, you traded with them. Mankind needed spear-points and sturdy spear-shafts, knapsacks and loin-straps, canteens and cooking vessels. You needed these articles and got them in exchange for heavy backloads of shapeless, unprocessed stuff freshly stolen. Mating with them—well, of course you mated with them. One was always on the lookout for extra women who could add to the knowledge and technical abilities of Mankind. But these women became a well-adjusted part of Mankind once they were stolen, just as Mankind's women were complete outsiders and Strangers the moment they had been carried off by a foreign raiding party. And fighting with them, warring with them—next to stealing from the Monsters, that was the sweetest, most exciting part of a warrior's existence.

You traded with Strangers, coldly, suspiciously, always alert for a better bargain; you stole Stranger women whenever you could, gleefully, proudly, because that diminished them and increased the numbers and well-being of Mankind; and you fought Stranger men whenever there was more to be gained that way than by simple trading—and periodically they came upon you as you lay in your burrow unawares and fought you.

But otherwise, for all normal social purposes, they were taboo. Almost as taboo and not-to-be-related-to as the Monsters on the other side of Mankind's burrows. When you came upon an individual Stranger wandering apart from his people, you killed him quickly and casually.

You certainly didn't ask him for advice on your Theft.

* * * * *

Eric was still brooding on the unprecedented nature of his uncle's instructions when they came to the end of their journey, a large, blind-alley burrow. There was a line cut deep into the blank wall here, a line that started at the floor, went up almost to the height of a man's head, and then curved down to the floor again.

The door to Monster territory.

Thomas the Trap-Smasher waited for a moment, listening. When his experienced ears had detected no unusual noises in the neighborhood, no hint of danger on the other side, he cupped his hands around his mouth, faced back the way he had come, and softly gave the ululating recognition-call of the band. The four other warriors and the apprentice came up swiftly and grouped themselves about him. Then, at a signal from their leader, all squatted near the door.

They ate first, rapidly and silently, removing from their knapsacks handfuls of food that the women had prepared for them and stuffing their mouths full, the beams from the glow lamps above their eyes darting incessantly back and forth along the arched, empty corridor. This was the place of ultimate, awful danger. This was the place where anything might happen.

Eric ate most sparingly of all as was correct for an initiate about to emerge upon his Theft. He knew he had to keep his springiness of body and watchfulness of mind at their highest possible pitch. He saw his uncle nodding approvingly as he returned the bulk of his food to the knapsack.

The floor vibrated slightly underfoot; there was a regular, rhythmic gurgling. Eric knew that meant they were directly over a length of Monster plumbing: upon his return, before the band started homewards, Thomas the Trap-Smasher would make an opening in the plumbing and they would refill their canteens. The water here, nearest to Monster territory, was always the sweetest and best.

Now his uncle got to his feet and called Roy the Runner to him. While the other warriors watched, tense and still, the two men walked to the curved line and laid their ears against it. Satisfied, finally, they inserted spear points into the door's outline on either side and carefully pried the slab back toward them. They laid it on the floor of the corridor, very gently.

A shimmering blur of pure whiteness appeared where the door had been.

Monster territory. The strange, alien light of Monster territory. Eric had seen many warriors disappear into it to fulfill their manhood tasks. Now it was his turn.

Holding his heavy spear at the ready, Eric's uncle leaned forward into the whiteness. His body twisted as he looked up, down, around, on both sides. He withdrew and came back into the burrow.

"No new traps," he said in a soft voice. "The one I dismantled last expedition is still up there on the wall. It hasn't been repaired. Now Eric. Here you go, boy."

Eric rose and walked with him to the doorway, remembering to keep his eyes on the floor. You can't look up, he had been told again and again, not right away, not the first time you're in Monster territory. If you do, you freeze, you're lost, you're done for completely.

His uncle checked him carefully and fondly, making certain that his new loin straps were tight, that his knapsack and back-sling were both in the right position on his shoulders. He took a heavy spear from Eric's right hand and replaced it with a light one from the back-sling. "If you're seen by a Monster," he whispered, "the heavy spear's not worth a damn. You scuttle into the closest hiding-place and throw the light spear as far as you can. The Monster can't distinguish between you and the spear. It will follow the spear."

Eric nodded mechanically, although this too he had been told many times, this too was a lesson he knew by heart. His mouth was so dry! He wished that it weren't unmanly to beg for water at such a moment.

Thomas the Trap-Smasher took his torch from him and slipped a glow lamp about his forehead. Then he pushed him through the doorway. "Go make your Theft, Eric," he whispered. "Come back a man."

THE MEN IN THE WALLS

IV

He was on the other side. He was in Monster territory. He was surrounded by the strange Monster light, the incredible Monster world. The burrows, Mankind, everything familiar, lay behind him.

Panic rose from his stomach and into his throat like vomit.

Don't look up. Eyes down, eyes down or you're likely to freeze right where you are. Stay close to the wall, keep your eyes on the wall and move along it. Turn right and move along the wall. Move fast.

Eric turned. He felt the wall brush his right shoulder. He began to run, keeping his eyes down, touching the wall with his shoulder at regular intervals. He ran as fast as he possibly could, urging his muscles fiercely on. As he ran, he counted the steps to himself.

Twenty paces. Where did the light come from? It was everywhere; it glowed so; it was white, white. *Twenty-five paces. Touch the wall with your shoulder. Don't—above everything—don't wander away from the wall. Thirty paces.* In light like this you had no need of the glow lamp. It was almost too bright to see in. *Thirty-five paces.* The floor was not like a burrow floor. It was flat and very hard. So was the wall. Flat and hard and straight. *Forty paces. Run and keep your eyes down. Run. Keep touching the wall with your shoulder. Move fast. But keep your eyes down. Don't look up. Forty-five paces.*

He almost smashed into the structure he had been told about, but his reflexes and the warnings he had received swung him to the left and along it just in time. It was a different color than the wall, he noted, and a different-textured material. *Keep your eyes down. Don't look up.* He came to an entrance, like the beginning of a small burrow.

Don't go in that first entrance, Eric; you pass it by. He began to count again as he ran. Twenty-three paces more, and there was another entrance, a much higher, wider one. He darted inside. *It'll be darker, at first. The walls will soak up light from your glow lamp.*

WILLIAM TENN

Eric paused, gasping. He was grateful for the sucking darkness. After that terrible, alien white light, the gloom was friendly, reminiscent of the familiar burrows now so horribly far away.

He could afford to take a breath at this point, he knew. The first, the worst part was over. He wasn't out in the open any more.

He had emerged into Monster territory. He had run fast, following instructions until he was safely under cover again. He was still alive.

The worst was over. Nothing else would be as bad as this.

Monster territory. It lay behind him, bathed in its own peculiar light. Now. Why not? Now, when he was in a place of comparative safety. He could take a chance. He *wanted* to take a chance.

He turned, gingerly, fearfully. He raised his eyes. He looked.

*   *   *   *   *

The cry that tore from his lips was completely involuntary and frightened him almost as much as what he saw. He shut his eyes and threw himself down and sideways. He lay where he had fallen for a long while, almost paralyzed.

It couldn't be. He hadn't seen it. Nothing was that high, nothing ran on and on for such incredible distances!

After a time, he opened his eyes again, keeping them carefully focused on the dark near him. The gloom in this covered place had diminished somewhat as his eyes had grown more accustomed to it. Yellowish light from his glow lamp was providing illumination now: he could make out the walls, about as far apart from each other as those in a burrow, but—unlike a burrow's walls—oddly straight and at right angles to the floor and ceiling. Far off there was an immense patch of darkness. *The burrow will open out into a great big space, a real big and real dark space.*

What was this place, he wondered? What was it to the Monsters?

He had to take another look behind, into the open. One more quick look. He was going to be Eric the Eye. An Eye should be able to look at anything. He had to take another look.

But guardedly, guardedly.

43

THE MEN IN THE WALLS

Eric turned again, opening his eyes a little at a time. He clamped his teeth together so as not to cry out. Even so, he almost did. He shut his eyes quickly, waited, then opened them again.

Bit by bit, effort by effort, he found he was able to look into the great open whiteness without losing control of himself. It was upsetting, overpowering, but if he didn't look too long at any one time, he could stand it.

Distance. Enormous, elongated, unbelievable distance. Space upon space upon space—that white light bathing it all. Space far ahead, space on all sides, space going on and on until it seemed to have no end to it at all. But there, fantastically far off, there was an end. There was a wall, a wall made by giants that finally sealed off the tremendous space. It rose hugely from the flat, huge floor and disappeared somewhere far overhead.

And in between—once you could stand to look at it this much—in between, there were objects. Enormous objects, dwarfed only by the greatness of the space which surrounded them, enormous, terribly alien objects. Objects like nothing you had ever imagined.

*   *   *   *   *

No, that wasn't quite true. That thing over there. Eric recognized it.

A great, squat thing like a full knapsack without the straps. Since early boyhood, many was the time he had heard it described by warriors back from an expedition into Monster territory.

There was food in that sack and the others like it. Enough food in that one sack to feed the entire population of Mankind for unnumbered auld lang synes. A different kind of food in each sack.

No spear point possessed by Mankind would cut through the fabric of its container, not near the bottom where it was thickest. Warriors had to climb about halfway up the sack, Eric knew, before they could find a place thin enough to carve themselves an entrance. Then the lumps of food would be lowered from man to man all the way down the sack, warriors clinging to precarious handholds every few paces.

WILLIAM TENN

Once the pile on the floor was great enough, they would clamber down and fill their specially large, food-expedition knapsacks. Then back to the burrows and to the women who alone possessed the lore of determining whether the food was fit for consumption and of preparing it if it were.

That's where he would be at this moment, on that sack, cutting a hole in it, if he'd chosen a first category Theft like most other youths. He'd be cutting a hole, scooping out a handful of food—any quantity, no matter how small, was acceptable on an initiatory Theft—and be preparing to go home to plaudits from the women and acceptance from the men. He'd be engaged in a normal, socially-acceptable endeavor.

Instead of which....

He found that he was able to stare at the Monster room now from under the cover of his hiding place with only a slight feeling of nausea. Well, that in itself was an achievement. After only a short time, here he was, able to look around and estimate the nature of Monster goods like the most experienced warrior. He couldn't look up too high as yet, but what warrior could?

Well and good, but this wasn't getting him anywhere. He didn't have a normal Theft to make. His was third category. Monster souvenirs.

Eric turned and faced the darkness again. He walked rapidly forward into the straight-walled burrow, the glow-lamp on his forehead lighting a yellow path. Ahead of him, the great black space grew steadily larger as he pushed towards it.

Everything about his Theft, his initiation into manhood, was extraordinary. Thomas the Trap-Smasher telling the women about his special talents, so that he would be accorded a vision and a name which would fit with them. Visions were supposed to come from the ancestors, through the Ancestor-science of the record machine. Nobody was supposed to have the slightest idea in advance of what the vision would be. That was all up to the ancestors and their mysterious plans for their descendants.

*   *   *   *   *

Was it possible, was it conceivable, that all visions and names were pre-arranged, that the record machine was set in advance for every initiation? Where did that leave religion? If that were so, how could you continue to believe in logic, in cause and effect?

And having someone—a Stranger, at that!—help you make your Theft. A Theft was supposed to be purely and simply a test of your male potential; by definition, it was something you did alone.

But if you could accept the concept of pre-arranged visions, why not pre-arranged Thefts?

Eric shook his head. He was getting into very dark corridors mentally: his world was turning into sheer confusion.

But one thing he knew. Making an arrangement with a Stranger, as his uncle had done, was definitely an act contrary to all the laws and practices of Mankind. Thomas's uncertain speech had underlined that fact. It was—well, it was *wrong*.

Yet his uncle was the greatest man in all Mankind, so far as Eric was concerned. Thomas the Trap-Smasher could do no wrong. But Thomas the Trap-Smasher was evidently leaning toward Alien-science. Alien-science was wrong. But again, on the other hand, his parents, according to the Trap-Smasher, his father and his mother had been Alien-sciencers.

Too much. There was just too much to work out. There was too much he didn't know. He'd better concentrate on his Theft.

The strange burrow had come to an end. The hairs rose on the back of his neck as he walked into the great dark area and sensed enormous black heights above him. He began to hurry, turning every once in a while to make certain that he was staying in a straight line with the light from the entrance. Here, his forehead glow lamp was almost no use at all. He didn't like this place. It felt almost like being out in the open.

WILLIAM TENN

What, he wondered again feverishly, was this structure in the world of the Monsters? What function did it have? He was not sure he wanted to know.

Eric was running by the time he came to the end of the open space. He hit the wall so hard that he was knocked over backwards.

For a moment, he was badly frightened, then he realized what had happened. He hadn't taken his bearings for a while: he must have moved off at an angle.

Groping along the wall with extended arms, he found the entrance to the low burrow at last. It was quite low—he had to bend his knees and duck his head as he went up to. It was an unpleasantly narrow little corridor. But then there was an opening on his right—the fork his uncle had told him about—and he turned into it with relief.

He had arrived.

There was a burst of light from a group of glow lamps. And there were Strangers, there were *several* Strangers here. Three of them—no, four—no, five! They squatted in a corner of this large, square burrow, three of them talking earnestly, the other two engaged in some incomprehensible task with materials that were mostly unfamiliar.

*   *   *   *   *

All of them leaped to their feet as he trotted in and deployed instantly in a wide semi-circle facing him. Eric wished desperately he had been holding two heavy spears instead of the single light one. With two heavy spears you had both a shield and a dangerous offensive weapon. A light spear was good for a single cast, and that was that.

He held it nevertheless in the throwing position above his shoulder and glared fiercely, as a warrior of Mankind should. If he had to throw, he decided, he would spring to one side immediately afterward and try to pluck the two heavy spears from his back-sling. But if they rushed him right now—

THE MEN IN THE WALLS

"Who are you?" asked a strong-faced, middle-aged man in the center of the semi-circle, his spear throbbing in an upraised arm. "What's your name—what's your people?"

"Eric the Only," Eric told him quickly. Then he remembered to add: "I'm destined to be Eric the Eye. My people are Mankind."

"He's expected, one of us," the middle-aged man told the others who immediately relaxed, slung their spears and went back to what they had been doing. "Welcome, Eric the Only of Mankind. Put up your spear and sit with us. I am Arthur the Organizer."

Eric gingerly dropped his spear into the back-sling. He studied the Stranger.

A man about as old as his uncle and not nearly as hefty, although well-muscled enough for normal warlike purposes. He wore the loin-straps of a full warrior, but—as if these were not enough honor for a man—he also wore straps laced about his chest and across his shoulders, though he was carrying no knapsack. This was the fashion of many Strangers, Eric knew, as was the strap at the back of the head that held the hair in a tight tail away from the eyes instead of letting it hang wild and free as the hair of a warrior should. And the straps were decorated with odd, incised designs—another weak and unmanlike Stranger fashion.

Who but Strangers, Eric thought contemptuously, would group up in so an alien place without setting sentries at either end of their burrow? Truly Mankind had good reason to despise them!

But this man was a leader, he realized, a born leader, with an even more self-assured air than Thomas the Trap-Smasher, captain of the best band in all Mankind. He was studying Eric in turn, with eyes that weighed carefully and then, having decided on the measure, made a definite placement, fitting Eric permanently into this plan or that plan. He looked like a man whose head was full of many plans, each one evolving inexorably through action to a predetermined end.

He took Eric's arm companionably and led him to where the others squatted and talked and worked. This was no tribal burrow of any sort: it was quite apparently a field headquarters—and Arthur the Organizer was Commander-in-Chief. "I met your uncle," he told Eric, "about a dozen auld lang synes ago, when he came to us on a trading expedition—back in our burrows, I mean. A fine man, your uncle, very progressive. He's attended our secret meetings regularly, and there's going to be an important place for him in the great burrows we will dig, in the new world we are making. He reminds me a lot of your father. But so do you, my boy, so do you."

"Did you know my father?"

   *   *   *   *   *

Arthur the Organizer smiled and nodded. "Very well. He could have been a great man. He gave his life for the Cause. Who among us will ever forget Eric the—the—Eric the Store-keeper or something, wasn't it?"

"The Storeroom-Stormer. His name was Eric the Storeroom-Stormer."

"Yes, of course. Eric the Storeroom-Stormer. An unforgettable name with us, and an unforgettable man. But that's another story; we'll talk about it some other time. You'll have to be getting back to your uncle very soon." He picked up a flat board covered with odd markings and studied it with his glow lamp.

"How do you like that?" one of the men working with the unfamiliar materials muttered to his neighbor. "You ask him his people, and he says, 'Mankind.' *Mankind!*"

The other man chuckled. "A front-burrow tribe. What the hell do you expect—sophistication? Each and every front-burrow tribe calls itself Mankind. As far as these primitives are concerned, the human race stops at their outermost burrow. Your tribe, my tribe—you know what they call us? Strangers. In their eyes, there's not too much difference between us and the Monsters."

"That's what I mean. They don't see us as fellow-men. They are narrow-minded savages. Who needs them?"

THE MEN IN THE WALLS

Arthur the Organizer glanced at Eric's face. He turned sharply to the man who had spoken last.

"I'll tell you who needs them, Walter," he said. "The Cause needs them. If the front-burrow tribes are with us, it means our main lines of supply to Monster territory are kept open. But we need every fighter we can get, no matter how primitive. Every single tribe has to be with us if Alien-science is to be the dominant religion of the burrows, if we're to avoid the fiasco of the last rising. We need front-burrow men for their hunting, foraging skills and back-burrow men for their civilized skills. We need everybody in this thing, especially now."

The man called Walter put down his work and scowled at Eric dubiously. He seemed to be totally unconvinced.

"These arrogant back-burrowers with their ornamented straps and unmilitary manners! Men from different tribes sitting around and talking, when—if they had any sense of propriety at all—they should be killing each other!"

Suddenly, the floor shook under him. He almost fell. He staggered back and forth, trying to grab at the spears in his back-sling. He finally got used to it, managed to find a solid footing in the upheaval. The spear he held vibrated in his hand.

     *   *   *   *   *

From far away came a series of ear-splitting thumps. The floor swung to their rhythm. "What is it?" he cried, turning to Arthur. "What's going on?"

"You've never heard a Monster walking before?" the Organizer asked him unbelievingly. "That's right—this is your Theft, your first time out. It's a Monster, boy. A Monster's moving around in the Monster larder, doing whatever Monsters do. They have a right, you know," he added with a smile. "It's their larder. We're just—visitors."

Eric noticed that none of the others seemed particularly concerned. He drew a deep breath and reslung his spear. How the floor and the walls shook! What a fantastic, enormous creature that must be!

50

WILLIAM TENN

As an apprentice warrior, he had often stood with the rear-guard on the other side of the doorway to Monster territory while the band went in to steal for Mankind. A few times there had been heavy, thumping noises off in the distance, and the walls of the burrow had quivered slightly. But not like this. It had never been remotely as awesome as this.

He raised his eyes to the straight, flat ceiling of the burrow above them. He remembered the dark space further back stretching up limitlessly. "And this," he said aloud. "This structure we're in. What is *this* to them?"

Arthur the Organizer shrugged. "A piece of Monster furniture. Something they use for something or other. We're in one of the open spaces they always leave in the bases of their furniture. Makes the furniture lighter, easier to move around, I guess." He listened for a moment as the thumps drifted further away and then died out. "Let's get down to business. Eric, this is Walter the Weapon-Seeker. Walter the Weapon-Seeker of the Miximilian people. Walter, what do you have for Eric's tribe—for, uh, for Mankind?"

"I hate to give anything even halfway good to a front-burrow tribe," the squatting man muttered. "No matter how much you explain it to them, they always use it wrong, they botch it up every single time. Let's see. This should be simple enough."

He rummaged in the pile of strange stuff in front of him and picked up a small, red, jelly-like blob. "All you do," he explained, "is tear off a pinch with your fingers. Just a pinch at a time, no more. Then spit on it and throw it. After you spit on it, get it out of your hands fast. Throw it as fast and as far as you can. Do you think you can remember that?"

"Yes." Eric took the red blob from him and stared at it in puzzlement. There was a strange, irritating odor: it made his nose itch slightly. "But what happens? What does it do?"

"That's not your worry, boy," Arthur the Organizer told him. "Your uncle will know when to use it. You have your third category theft—a

51

Monster souvenir that no one in your tribe has ever seen before. It should make them sit up and take notice. And tell your uncle to bring his band to my burrow three days—three sleep-periods—from now. That will be the last time we meet before the rising. Tell him to bring them armed with every last spear they can carry."

*   *   *   *   *

Eric nodded weakly. There were so many complex, incomprehensible things going on! The world was a bigger, more active place than he had ever imagined.

He watched Arthur the Organizer add a mark to the flat board on which many symbols were scratched. This was another Stranger practice—made necessary, he knew, by the weak Stranger memory, so inferior to that of Mankind.

The Weapon-Seeker leaped up and stopped him as he was about to put the red blob into his knapsack. "Nothing wet in there?" Walter demanded, opening the bag and rummaging about in Eric's belongings. "No water? Remember, get this stuff wet and you're done for."

"Mankind keeps its water in canteens," Eric explained irritably. "We keep it here," he pointed to the sloshing pouch at his hip, "not splashing around loosely with our provisions." He swung the full knapsack on his back and stepped away with stiff dignity.

Arthur the Organizer accompanied him to the end of the burrow. "Don't mind Walter," he whispered. "He's always afraid that nobody but himself will be able to use the Monster weapons he digs up. He talks that way to everyone. Now, suppose I refresh your memory about the way back. We don't want you to get lost."

"I won't get lost," Eric said coldly. "I have a good memory, and I know enough to perform a simple reversal of the directions on the way here. Besides, I am Eric the Espier, Eric the Eye of Mankind. I won't get lost."

He was rather proud of himself as he trotted away, without turning his head. Let the Strangers know what you think of them. The snobs. The stuck-up bastards.

But still, he felt damaged somehow, made less—as when Roy the Runner had called him a singleton before the entire band. And the last comment he had heard behind him—"These primitives: so damned touchy!"—made it no better.

He crossed the dark open space, still brooding, his eyes fixed on the patch of white light ahead, his mind engaged in a completely unaccustomed examination of values. Mankind's free simplicity against the Stranger multiplicity and intricacy. Mankind's knowledge of basics, the important foraging basics of day-to-day life, against the Stranger knowledge of so many things and techniques he had never even heard about. Surely Mankind's way was infinitely preferable, far superior?

Then why did his uncle want to get mixed up with Stranger politics, he wondered, as he emerged from the structure? He turned left and, passing the small entrance he had ignored before, sped for the wall which separated him from the burrows. And why did all these Strangers, evidently each from a different tribe, agree in the contempt with which they held Mankind?

He had just turned right along the wall, on the last stretch before the doorway, when the floor shook again, jarring him out of his thoughts. He bounced up and down, frozen with fear where he stood.

He was out in the open while a Monster was abroad. A Monster had come into the larder again.

V

Far off in the dazzling distance, he caught sight of the tremendously long gray body he had heard about since childhood, higher than a hundred men standing on each other's shoulders, the thick gray legs each wider than two hefty men standing chest to chest. He caught just one wide-eyed, fear-soluble glimpse of the thing before he went into complete panic.

His panic was redeemed by a single inhibition: he didn't spring forward and run away from the wall. But that was only because it would have meant running directly toward the Monster. For one thoroughly insane moment, however, he thought of trying to claw his way through the wall against which his shoulders were pressed.

Then—because it was the direction he had been running in—he remembered the doorway. He must be about thirty, thirty-five paces from it. There lay safety: his uncle, the band, Mankind and the burrows—the blessed, closed-in, narrow burrows!

Eric leaped along the wall for the doorway. He ran as he'd never in his life run before, as he'd never imagined he could run.

But even as he fled madly, almost weeping at the effort he was making, a few sane thoughts—the result of long, tiresome drills as an initiate—organized themselves in his screaming mind. He had been closer to the structure in which the Strangers were hiding the structure which Arthur the Organizer explained was a piece of Monster furniture. He should have turned the other way, towards the structure, gotten between it and the wall. There, unless he'd been seen as the Monster entered the larder, he could have rested safely until it was possible to make his escape.

He had gone too far to turn back now. But run silently, he reminded himself: run swiftly but make no noise, make no noise at all. According to the lessons that the warriors taught, at this distance Monster hearing was more to be feared than Monster vision. Run silently. Run for your life.

He reached the door. It had been set back in place!

In disbelief and utter horror he stared at the curved line in the wall that showed where the door had been replaced in its socket. But this was never done! This had never been heard of!

WILLIAM TENN

Eric beat frantically on the door with his fists. Would his knuckles make enough noise to penetrate the heavy slab? Or just enough to attract the Monster's attention?

He twisted his head quickly—a look, a deliberately wasted moment, to estimate the closeness of his danger. The Monster's legs moved so slowly: its speed would have been laughable if the very size of those legs didn't serve to push it forward an incredible distance with each step. And there was nothing laughable in that long, narrow neck, almost as long as the rest of the body, and the malevolent, relatively tiny head on the end of the neck. And those horrible pink things, all around the neck, just behind the head—

It was much nearer than it had been just seconds ago, but whether it had noticed him and was coming at him he had no idea. Beat at the door with the shaft of a spear? That should attract attention, that might be heard.

Yes, by the Monster too.

*   *   *   *   *

There was only one thing to do. He stepped a few paces back from the wall. Then he leaped forward, smashing his shoulder into the door. He felt it give a little. Another try.

The floor-shaking thumps of the Monster's steps were now so close as to be almost deafening. At any moment, a great gray foot might come down and grind out his life. Eric stepped back again, forcing himself not to look up.

Another leap, another bruising collision with the door. It had definitely moved. An indentation showed all around it.

Was he about to be stepped on—to be squashed?

Eric put his hands on the door. He pushed. Slowly, suckingly, it left the place out of which it had been carved long ago.

Where was the Monster? How close? How Close?

Suddenly, the door fell over into the burrow, and Eric spilled painfully on top of it. He scrambled to his feet and darted down the corridor.

THE MEN IN THE WALLS

He had no time to feel relief. His mind was repeating its lessons, reminding him what he had to do next in such a situation.

Run a short distance down the burrow. Then stop and wait on the balls of your feet, ready to bolt. Get as much air into your lungs as possible. You may need it. If you hear a hissing, whistling sound, stop breathing and start running. Hold your breath for as long as you can—as long as you possibly can—then suck another chestful of air and keep running. Keep this up until you are far away. Far, far away.

Eric waited, poised to run, his back to the doorway.

Don't look around—just face the direction you'll have to run. There's only one thing you have to worry about, only one thing you have to listen for. A hissing, whistling sound. When you hear it, hold your breath and run.

He waited, his muscles contracted for instant action.

Time went by. He remembered to count. If you counted up to five hundred, slowly, and nothing happened, you were likely to be all right. You could assume the Monster probably hadn't noticed you.

So the experienced warriors said, the men who had lived through such an experience.

Five hundred. He reached five hundred and, just to be on the safe side, still tense, still ready to run, counted another five hundred, up to the ultimate number conceived by man, a full thousand.

No hissing, no whistling sounds. No suggestion of danger.

He relaxed, and his muscles—suddenly set free—gave way. He fell to the floor of the burrow, whimpering with the release of tension.

It was over. His Theft was over. He was a man.

*   *   *   *   *

He had been in the same place as a Monster, and lived through it. He had met Strangers and dealt with them as a representative of Mankind. Such things as he would have to tell his uncle!

His uncle. Where was his uncle? Where was the band?

Suddenly fully aware of how much was wrong, Eric scrambled to his feet and walked cautiously back to the open doorway. The burrow was empty. They hadn't waited for him.

But that was another incredible thing! A band never gave an initiate up for lost until at least two full days had gone by. In the chief's absence, of course, this was measured by the sleep periods of the band captain. Any band would wait two days before giving up and turning homeward. And, Eric was positive, his uncle would have waited a bit longer than that for *him*. He'd been away for such a short time! Then what had happened?

He crept to the doorway and peeped outside. There was almost no dizziness this time. His eyes adjusted quickly to the different scale of distance. The Monster was busy on the other side of the larder. It had merely been crossing the room, then, not pursuing and attacking. Apparently it hadn't noticed him at all.

Fantastic. And with all the noise he had made! All that rushing back and forth, that battering-down of the door!

The Monster turned abruptly, walked a few gigantic steps and hurled itself at the structure in which Eric had met the Strangers. The walls, the floor, everything, shook mightily in sympathy to the impact of the great organism as it wriggled a bit and became still.

Eric was startled until he realized that the creature had done no more than lie down in the structure. It *was* a piece of Monster furniture, after all.

How had that felt to Arthur the Organizer and Walter the Weapon-Seeker and the others hidden in the base? Eric grinned. Those Strangers must be a little less haughty, a little more sober at this moment.

Meanwhile, he had work to do, things to find out.

He got his fingers under the slab of door and tugged it upright. It was heavy! He pushed against it, slowly, carefully, first one side and then the other, walking it back to the hole in the wall. A final push, and it slid into place tightly, only the thin, curved line suggesting its existence.

Now he could look around.

There had been a fight here—that much was certain. A brief, bitter battle. Examining the area closely, Eric saw unmistakable signs of conflict.

A broken spear shaft. Some blood on the wall. Part of a torn knapsack. No bodies, of course. You were not likely to find bodies after a battle. Any people of the burrows knew that the one unavoidable imperative of victory was to drag the bodies away and dispose of them. No one might ever leave dead enemies to rot where they would foul the corridors.

*　　*　　*　　*　　*

So there had been a battle. He had been right—his uncle and his uncle's band had not just gone off and left him. There must have been an attack by a superior force. The band had stood its ground for a while, sustained some losses, and then been forced to retreat.

But there were a few things which didn't make sense. First, it was very unusual for a war party of Strangers to come this close to Monster territory. The burrows which were inhabited by Mankind, the natural goal of a war party, were much further back. At this point, you would not expect to find any group larger than a foraging expedition—a Stranger band at most.

His uncle's men, fully armed, operating under battle alert, could easily cope with a single band of weavers, weaponsmiths or traders from the decadent back-burrows. They would have driven them off, possibly taking a few prisoners, and continued to wait for him.

That left only two possibilities. The unlikely war party—a two or three-band attack—and, even more unlikely, a band from another fierce, front-burrow people. But front-burrowers rarely went prowling at random near Monster territory. They would have their own door cut into it and would tend to feel hugely uncertain about one belonging to another people. They too would head for the inhabited burrows if they were on any business other than the important one of stealing for their tribe's needs.

And another thing. Unless his uncle's band had been wiped out to the very last man—a thought Eric rejected as highly improbable—the survivors were honor-bound, by their oath of manhood, after doing whatever the immediate military situation required, from pursuit to retreat, to return as soon as possible to the spot where an initiate was expected back from his Theft. No warrior would dare face the women if he failed to do this.

Possibly the attack had just come. Possibly his uncle's band was a short distance away, still fighting their way from burrow's end to burrow's end; and, once they had gotten clear of the enemy, would make their way back to him.

No. In that case, he should be able to hear the battle still going on. And the burrows were dreadfully still.

Eric shivered. A warrior was not meant to be abroad without companions. He'd heard of tribeless Strangers—once, as a child, he remembered enjoying the intricate execution of a man who'd been expelled from his own people for some major crime and who had wandered pathetically into the neighborhood of Mankind—but these people were hardly to be considered human: tribes, bands, societies, were the surroundings of human creatures.

It was awful to be alone. It was unthinkable.

*　　*　　*　　*　　*

Without bothering to eat, though he was quite hungry after his Theft, he began walking rapidly down the corridor. After a while, he broke into a trot. He wanted to get home as soon as possible—to be among his own kind again.

He reached into his back-sling and got a spear for each hand.

A nervous business going through the corridors all by yourself. They were so empty and so quiet. They hadn't seemed this quiet when he'd been on expedition with the band. And so fearfully, frighteningly dim. Eric had never before realized how much difference there was between the light you got from one forehead glow-lamp and the usual band complement of a half-dozen. He found himself getting more and more wary of the unexpected shadows where the wall curved sharply: he picked up speed as he ran past the black hole of a branching burrow.

At any one of those places, an enemy could be waiting for him, warned by the sound of his approaching footsteps. It could be the same enemy which had attacked his uncle's band, a handful of cruel and murderous Strangers, or a horde of them. It could be something worse. Abruptly he remembered legends of unmentionable creatures who lurked in the empty burrows, creatures who fled before the approach of a band of warriors, but who would come noiselessly upon a single man. Big creatures who engulfed you. Tiny creatures who came in their hundreds and nibbled you to pieces. Eric kept jerking his head around to look behind him: at least he could keep his doom from taking him by surprise.

It was *awful* to be alone.

And yet, in the midst of his fears, his mind returned again and again to the problem of his uncle's disappearance. Eric could not believe anything serious had happened to him. Thomas the Trap-Smasher was a veteran of too many bloody adventures, too many battles against unequal odds. Then where had he gone? And where had he taken the band?

And why was there no sound of him anywhere, no sign in all this infinity of gloomy, stretching, menace-filled tunnels?

Fortunately, he was an Eye. He knew the way back and sped desperately along it without the slightest feeling of doubt. The Record Machine was right: he would never be lost. Let him just get safely back to the companionship of Mankind and he would be Eric the Eye.

And there it was again: who had been right, the Record Machine or his uncle? The vision that named him had come from the Record Machine, but his uncle claimed that this was religious claptrap. The vision had been selected and his name proposed to the women well in advance of the ceremony. And his uncle was an Alien-sciencer, in touch with Strangers who were also Alien-sciencers....

So many things had happened in the last two days, Eric felt. So much of his world had shifted. It was as if the walls of the burrows had moved outward and upward until they resembled Monster territory more than human areas.

*   *   *   *   *

He was getting close now. These corridors looked friendlier, more familiar. He made himself run faster, although he was almost at the point of exhaustion. He wanted to be home, to be officially Eric the Eye, to inform Mankind of what had happened so that a rescue and searching party could be sent out for his uncle.

That doorway to Monster territory: who had replaced it? If a battle had been fought, and his uncle's band had retreated, still fighting, would the attacker have stopped to put the door neatly back in its socket? No.

Could it be explained by a sudden onslaught and the complete extermination of his uncle's band? Then, before dragging the bodies away, the enemy would have had time to put the door back. A doorway into Monster territory was a valuable human resource, after all, valuable to Mankind and Strangers alike—why jeopardize it by leaving it visible and open?

But who—or what—could have been capable of such a sudden onslaught, such a complete extermination of the best-led band in all Mankind? He'd have to get the answer from one of the other band captains or possibly a wise old crone in the Female Society.

Definitely within the boundaries of Mankind now, Eric forced himself to slow to a walk. He would be coming upon a sentry at any moment, and he had no desire at all to have a spear flung through him. A sentry would react violently to a man dashing out of the darkness.

"Eric the Only," he called out, identifying himself with each step. "This is Eric the Only." Then he remembered his Theft proudly and changed the identification. "Eric the Eye. This is Eric the Eye, the Espier, the further-seeing, less-paying Eye. Eric the Eye is coming back to Mankind!"

Oddly, there was no returning call of recognition. Eric didn't understand that. Had Mankind itself been attacked and driven away from its burrow? A sentry should respond to a familiar name. Something was very, inexplicably wrong.

Then he came around the last curve and saw the sentry at the other end. Rather, he saw what at first looked like three sentries. They were staring at him, and he recognized them. Stephen the Strong-Armed and two members of Stephen's band. Evidently he had arrived just at the moment when the sentry on duty was about to be relieved. That would account for Stephen and the other man. But why hadn't they replied to his shouts of identification?

They stood there silently as he came up, their spears still at the ready, not going down in welcome. "Eric the Eye," he repeated, puzzled. "I've made my Theft, but something happened to the rest—"

His voice trailed off, as Stephen came up to him, his face grim, his powerful muscles taut. The band captain shoved a spear point hard against Eric's chest. "Don't move," he warned. "Barney. John. Tie him up. We've caught the little rat!"

VI

His spears taken from him, his arms bound securely behind his back by the thongs of his own knapsack, Eric was pushed and prodded into the great central burrow of Mankind.

The place was almost unrecognizable.

Under the direction of Ottilie, the Chieftain's First Wife, a horde of women—what seemed at first like the entire membership of the Female Society—was setting up a platform in front of the Royal Mound. With the great scarcity of any building materials that

Mankind suffered from, a construction of this sort was startling and unusual, yet there was something about it that awoke highly unpleasant memories in Eric's mind. But he was pulled from place to place too fast and there were too many other unprecedented things going on for him to be able to identify the memory properly.

Two women who were accredited members of the Female Society were not working under Ottilie's direction, he noticed. Bound hand and foot, they were lying against the far wall of the great central burrow. They were both covered with blood and showed every sign of having undergone prolonged and most vicious torture. He judged them to be barely this side of death.

As he was jerked past, he recognized them. They were the two wives of Thomas the Trap-Smasher.

Just wait until his uncle got back! Someone would really pay for this, he thought, more in absolute amazement than horror. He had the feeling that he must keep the horror away at all costs. Once let it in and it would soak through his thoughts right into the memory he was trying to avoid.

The place was full of armed men, running back and forth from their band captains to unknown destinations in the outlying corridors. Between them and around them scuttled the children, fetching and carrying raw materials for the hard-working women. There was a steady buzz of commands in the air ... "Go to—" "Bring some more—" "Hurry with the—" ... that mingled with the smell of many people whose pores were sweating urgency. And it wasn't just sweat that he smelled. Eric realized as he was dragged before the Royal Mound. It was anger. The anger and fear of all Mankind.

Franklin the Father of Many Thieves stood on the mound, carrying unaccustomed spears in his fat hands, talking rapidly to a group of warriors, band captains and—yes, actually!—*Strangers.* Even now, Eric found he could still be astonished at this fantastic development.

Strangers in the very midst of Mankind! Walking around freely and bearing arms!

THE MEN IN THE WALLS

As the chief caught sight of Eric, his face broke into a loose-skinned smile. He nudged a Stranger beside him and pointed at the prisoner.

"That's him," he said. "That's the nephew. The one that asked for the third category Theft. Now we've got them all."

The Stranger didn't smile. He looked briefly at Eric and turned away. "I'm glad you think so. From our point of view, you've just got one more."

* * * * *

Franklin's smile faded to an uncertain grin. "Well, you know what I mean. And the damned fool came back by himself. It saved us a lot of trouble, I mean, didn't it?" Receiving no answer, he shrugged. He gestured with flabby imperiousness at Eric's guards. "You know where to put him. We'll be ready for them pretty soon."

Again the point of a spear stabbed into Eric's back, and he was forced forward across the central space to a small burrow entrance. Before he could reach it, however, he heard Franklin the Father of Many Thieves call out to Mankind: "There goes Eric, my people. Eric the Only. Now we've got the last of the filthy gang!"

For a moment, the activity stopped and seemed to focus on him. Eric shivered as a low, drawn-out grunt of viciousness and hatred arose everywhere, but most of all from the women.

Someone ran up to him. Harriet the History-Teller. The girl's face was absolutely contorted. She reached up to the crown of her head and pulled out the long pin held in place by a few knotted scarlet hairs. About her face and neck the hair danced like flames.

"You Alien-sciencer!" she shrieked, driving the pin straight at his eyes. "You filthy, filthy Alien-sciencer!"

Eric whipped his head to one side; she was back at him in a moment. His guards leaped at the girl and grappled with her, but she was able to get in one ripping slash that opened up almost all of his right cheek before they drove her away.

"Leave something for the rest of us," one of his guards pleaded the cause of reason as he strolled back to Eric. "After all, he belongs to the whole of Mankind."

"He does not!" she yelled. "He belongs to me most of all. I was going to mate with him when he returned from his Theft, wasn't I, Mother?"

"There wasn't anything official," Eric heard Rita the Record-Keeper admonishing as he tried to stanch the flow of blood by bringing his shoulder up and pressing it against the wound. "There couldn't be anything official about it until he'd achieved manhood. So you'll just have to wait your turn, Harriet, darling. You'll have to wait until your elders are finished with him. There'll be plenty left for you."

"There won't be," the girl pouted. "I know what you're like. There won't be hardly anything left."

Eric was shoved at the small burrow entrance again. The moment he was inside it, one of his guards planted a foot in his back, knocking the breath out of him. The kick propelled him forward, staggering wildly for balance, until he smashed into the opposite wall. As he fell, unable to use his arms to cushion himself, he heard laughter behind him in the great central burrow. He rolled on his side dizzily. There was a fresh flow of blood coming down from his cheek.

This wasn't the homecoming he'd imagined after his Theft—not in the slightest! What was going on?

He knew where he was. A tiny, blind-alley burrow off Mankind's major meeting-place, a sort of little vault used mostly for storage. Excess food and goods stolen from Monster territory were kept here until there was enough accumulated for a trading expedition to the back burrows. Occasionally, also, a male Stranger, taken prisoner in battle, might be held in this place until Mankind found out if his tribe valued him enough to pay anything substantial for his recovery.

And if they didn't....

THE MEN IN THE WALLS

* * * * *

Eric remembered the unusual structure that the women had been building near the Royal Mound—and shivered. The memory that he'd suppressed had now come alive in his mind. And it fitted with the way Harriet had acted—and with what her mother, Rita the Record-Keeper, had said.

They couldn't be planning that for him! He was a member of Mankind, almost a full warrior. They didn't even do that to Strangers captured in battle—not *normal* Strangers. A warrior was always respected as a warrior. At the worst, he deserved a decent execution, quietly done. Except for—Except for—

"*No!*" he screamed. "*No!*"

The single guard who'd been left on duty at the entrance turned around and regarded him humorously.

"Oh, yes," he said. "Oh, definitely yes! We're going to have a lot of fun with both of you, as soon as the women say they're ready." He nodded with ominous, emphatic slowness and turned back to miss none of the preparations.

Both of you? For the first time, Eric looked around the little storage burrow. The place was almost empty of goods, but off to one side, in the light of his forehead glow-lamp (how proud he had been when it had been bestowed on him at the doorway to Monster territory!) he now saw another man lying bound against the wall.

His uncle.

Eric brought his knees up and wriggled rapidly over to him. It was a painful business. His belly and sides were not calloused and inured to the rough burrow floor like his feet. But what did a few scratches more or less matter any more?

The Trap-Smasher was barely conscious. He had been severely handled, and he looked almost as bad as his wives. There was a thick crust of dried blood on his hair. The haft of a spear, Eric guessed, had all but cracked his head open. And in several places on his body, his

66

right shoulder, just above his left hip, deep in his thigh, were the oozing craters of serious spear wounds, raw and unbandaged.

"Uncle Thomas," Eric urged. "What happened? Who did this to you?"

*   *   *   *   *

The wounded man opened his eyes and shuddered. He looked around stupidly as if he had expected to find the walls talking to him. And his powerful arms struggled with the knots that held them firmly behind his back. When he finally located Eric, he smiled.

It was a bad thing to do. Someone had also smashed in most of his front teeth.

"Hello, Eric," he mumbled. "What a fight, eh? How did the rest of the band do? Anybody get away?"

"I don't know. That's what I'm asking you! I came back from my Theft—you were gone—the band was gone. I got here, and everyone's crazy! There are Strangers out there, walking around with weapons in our burrows. Who are they?"

Thomas the Trap-Smasher's eyes had slowly darkened. They were fully in focus now, and long threads of agony swam in them. "Strangers?" he asked in a low voice. "Yes, there were Strangers fighting in Stephen the Strong-Armed's band. Fighting against us. That chief of ours—Franklin—he got in touch with Strangers after we left. They compared notes. They must have been working together, been in touch with each other, for a long time. Mankind, Strangers, what difference does it make when their lousy Ancestor-science is threatened? I should have remembered."

"What?" Eric begged. "What should you have remembered?"

"That's the way they put down Alien-science in the other rising, long ago. A chief's a chief. He's got more in common with another chief—even a chief of Strangers—than with his own people. You attack Ancestor-science, and you're attacking their power as chiefs. They'll work together then. They'll give each other men, weapons, information. They'll do everything they can against the common enemy. Against the only people who really want to hit back at the Monsters. I should have remembered! Damn it all," the Trap-Smasher groaned through his ruined mouth, "I saw that the chief and Ottilie were suspicious. I should have realized how they were going to handle it. They were going to call in Strangers, exchange information—and unite against us!"

Eric stared at his uncle, dimly understanding. Just as there was a secret organization of Alien-sciencers that cut across tribal boundaries, so there was a tacit, rarely-used understanding among the chiefs, based on the Ancestor-science religion that was the main prop of their power. *And* the power of the leaders of the Female Society, come to think of it. All special privileges were derived from their knowledge of Ancestor-science. Take that away from them, and they'd be ordinary women with no more magical abilities than was necessary to tell edible food from Monster poison.

Grunting with pain, Thomas the Trap-Smasher wormed his way up to a sitting position against the wall. He kept shaking his head as if to jar recollection loose.

"They came up to us," he said heavily, "Stephen the Strong-Armed and his band came up to us just after you'd gone into Monster territory. A band from Mankind with a message from the chief—who suspected anything? They might be coming to tell us that the home burrows were under attack by Strangers. Strangers!" He gave a barking laugh, and some blood splashed out of his mouth. "They had Strangers with them, hidden all the way behind in the corridors. Mobs and mobs of Strangers."

$*$ $*$ $*$ $*$ $*$

Eric began to visualize what had happened.

"Then, when they were among us, when most of us had reslung our spears, they hit us. Eric, they hit us real good. They had us so much by surprise that they didn't even need outside help. I don't think there was much left of us by the time the Strangers came running up. I was down, fighting with my bare hands, and so was the rest of the band. The Strangers did the mopping up. I didn't see most of it. Somebody handed me one hell of a wallop—I never expected to wake up alive." His voice got even lower and huskier. "I'd have been lucky not to."

The Trap-Smasher's chest heaved: a strange, long noise came out of it. "They brought me back here. My wives—they were working on my wives. Those bitches from the Female Society—Ottilie, Rita—this part of it is their business—they had my wives pegged out and they worked on them in front of me. I was blanking out and coming to, blanking out and coming to; I was conscious while they—"

He dropped to a bloody mumble again, his head falling forward loosely. His voice became clear for a moment, but not entirely rational. "They were good women," he muttered. "Both of them. Good, good girls. And they loved me. They had their chance to become more important. A dozen times Franklin must have offered to impregnate them, and they turned him down every time. They really loved me."

Eric almost sobbed himself. He'd had little to do with them once he'd reached the age of the warrior initiate, but in his childhood, they'd given him all the mother love he ever remembered. They'd cuffed him and caressed him and wiped his nose. They'd told him stories and taught him the catechism of the ancestral science. Neither had sons of his age who had survived the various plagues and the Monster-inflicted calamities that periodically swept through Mankind's burrows. He'd been lucky. He'd received much of the care and affection that their own sons might have enjoyed.

Their fidelity to the Trap-Smasher had been a constant source of astonishment in Mankind. It had cost them more than the large, healthy litters for which the chief had a well proven capacity: such eccentric, almost non-womanly behavior had inevitably denied them the high positions in the Female Society they would otherwise have enjoyed.

THE MEN IN THE WALLS

And now they were dead or dying, and their surviving babies had been apportioned to other women whose importance would thereby be substantially increased.

"Tell me," he asked his uncle. "Why did the Female Society kill them? What did they do that was so awful?"

He saw that Thomas had lifted his head again and was staring at him. With pity. He felt his own body turn completely cold even before the Trap-Smasher spoke.

"You still won't let yourself think about it? I don't blame you, Eric. But it's there. It's being prepared for us outside."

"What?" Eric demanded, although a distant part of him had already worked out the terrible answer and knew what it was.

"We've been declared outlaws, Eric. They say we're guilty of the ultimate sacrilege against Ancestor-Science. We don't belong to Mankind anymore—you, me, my family, my band. We're outside Mankind, outside the law, outside religion. And you know what happens to outlaws, Eric, don't you? Anything goes. *Anything.*"

VII

Ever since early childhood, Eric remembered looking forward to ceremonies of this sort. A Stranger would have been caught by one of the warrior bands, and it would be determined that he was an outlaw. Nine times out of ten, such a man was easy enough to identify. No one but an outlaw, for example, would be wandering the burrows by himself, without a band or at least a single companion to guard his back. The tenth time, when there was the slightest doubt, a request for ransom to his people would make the prisoner's position clear. There would be a story of some unforgivable sacrilege, some particularly monstrous crime that could be punished by nothing but complete anathema and the revocation of all privileges as a human being. The man had escaped the punishment being prepared for him. Do with him as you will, his people would say. He is no longer one of us; he is the same as a Monster; he is something non-human so far as we are concerned.

Then a sort of holiday would be declared. Out of the bits and pieces of lumber stolen from Monster territory and set aside by the women for this purpose, the members of the Female Society would erect a structure whose specifications had been handed down from mother to daughter for countless generations—all the way back to the ancestors who had built the Record-Machines. It was called a Stage or a Theater, although Eric had also heard it referred to as The Scaffold. In any case, whatever its true name, most of the details concerning it were part of the secret lore of the Female Society and, as such, were no proper concern of males.

One thing about it, however, everyone knew. On it would be enacted a moving religious drama: the ultimate triumph of humanity over the wickedness of the Monsters.

For this, the central character had to fulfill two requirements. He had to be an intelligent creature, as the Monsters were, so that he could be made to suffer as some day Mankind meant the Monsters to suffer; and he had to be non-human, as the Monsters were, so that every drop of fear, resentment and hatred distilled by the enormous swaggering aliens could be poured out upon his flesh without any inhibition of compunction or fellow-feeling.

For this purpose, outlaws were absolutely ideal, since all agreed that such disgusting creatures had resigned their membership in the human race.

*   *   *   *   *

When an outlaw was caught, work stopped in the burrows, and Mankind's warrior bands were called home. It was a great time, a joyous time, a time of festival. Even the children—doing whatever they could to prepare for the glorious event, running errands for the laboring women, fetching refreshment for the stalwart, guarding men—even the children boasted to each other of how they would express their hatred upon this trapped representative of the non-human, this bound and shrieking protagonist of the utterly alien.

Everyone had their chance. All, from the chief himself to the youngest child capable of reciting the catechism of ancestral science, all climbed in their turn upon the Stage—or Theater—or Scaffold—that the women had erected. All were thrilled to vent a portion of Mankind's vengeance upon the creature who had been declared alien, as an earnest of what they would some day do collectively to the Monsters who had stolen their world.

Sarah the Sickness-Healer had her turn early in the proceedings; thenceforth, she stood on the structure and carefully supervised the ceremony. It was her job to see that nobody went too far, that everyone had a fair and adequate turn, and that even at the end there was some life left in the victim. Because then, at the end, the structure had to be completely burned—along with its bloody occupant—as a symbol of how the Monsters must eventually be turned into ash and be blown away and vanish.

"*And Mankind will come into its own,*" she would chant, while the charred fragments were kicked out of the burrow contemptuously. "*And the Monsters will be gone. They will be gone forever, and there will be nothing upon all the wide Earth but Mankind.*"

Afterwards, there was feasting, there was dancing, there was singing. Men and women chased each other into the dimmer side corridors; children whooped and yelled around the great central burrow; the few old folks went to sleep with broad, reminiscent smiles upon their faces. Everyone felt they had somehow struck back at the Monsters. Everyone felt a little like the lords of creation their ancestors had been.

Eric remembered the things he himself had done—the things he had seen others do—on these occasions. A tremendous tic of fear rippled through his body. He had to draw his shoulders up to his neck in a tight hunch and tense the muscles of his arms and legs. Finally his nerves subsided.

He could think again. Only he didn't want to think.

Those others, those outlaws in previous ceremonies of this sort in auld lang synes long past—was it possible that they had experienced the same sick, bewildered dread while waiting for the structure to be completed? Had they trembled like this, had they also felt wetness running down their backs, had they felt the same pleading squirm in their intestines, the same anticipatory twinges of soft, vulnerable flesh?

*   *   *   *   *

The thought had never crossed his mind before. He'd seen them as things completely outside humanity, the compressed symbol of all that was alien. One worried about their feelings no more than about those of the roaches scurrying madly about here in the storage burrow. One squashed them slowly or rapidly—at one's pleasure. What difference did it make? You didn't sympathize with roaches. You didn't identify with them.

But now that he was about to be squashed himself, he realized that it did make a difference. He was human. No matter what Mankind and its leaders now declared him to be, he was human. He felt human fears; he experienced a desperate human desire to live.

Then so had the others been. The outlaws whom he'd helped tear to pieces. Human. Completely human.

They'd sat here, just as he did now, they'd sat and waited for the festival and its agonies....

Only twice in his memory had members of Mankind ever been declared outlaw. Both cases had occurred a long time ago, before he'd even been a warrior-initiate. Eric tried now to remember what they had been like as living people. He wanted to reach out and feel companionship, some sort of companionship, even that of the dead. The dead were better than this beaten, bloody man next to him who had subsided into half-insane mumbles, his battered head on his torn and wound-scribbled chest.

THE MEN IN THE WALLS

What had they been like? It was no use. In the first case, memory brought back only a picture of a screaming hulk just before the fire was lit. No recollection of a man. No fellow-human in Mankind. And in the second case—

Eric sat bolt upright, straining against his bonds. The second man to be declared an outlaw had escaped! How he had done it Eric had never found out: he remembered only that a guard was severely punished, and that bands of warriors had sniffed for him along far-distant corridors for a long time afterward.

Escape. That was it. He had to escape. Once declared an outlaw, he could have no hope of mercy, no remission of sentence. The religious overtones of the ceremony being prepared were too highly charged to be halted for anything short of the disappearance of its chief protagonist.

Yes, escape. But how? Even if he could get free of the knots which so expertly and so strongly tied his hands behind his back, he had no weapon to hand. The guard at the entrance would transfix him with a spear in a moment. And if he failed, there were others outside, almost the entire warrior strength of the people.

How? *How?* He forced himself to be calm, to go over every possible alternative in his mind. He knew there was not much time. In a little while, the structure would be finished and the leaders of the Female Society would come for him.

      *   *   *   *   *

Eric began working on the knots behind him. He worked without much hope. If he could get his hands loose, perhaps he might squirm his way carefully to the entrance, leap up suddenly and break into a run. So what if they threw a spear through him—wouldn't that be better and quicker than the other thing?

But they wouldn't, he realized. Not unless he were very lucky and some warrior forgot to think straight. In cases like this, when it was a matter of keeping, not killing a prisoner, you aimed for the legs. There were at least a dozen men in Mankind with skill great enough to bring him down even at twenty or twenty-five paces. And another dozen who might be able to catch him. He was no Roy the Runner, after all.

Roy! He was dead and sewered by now. He found himself regretting the fight he'd had with Roy.

A Stranger passed by the storage burrow entrance, glancing in with only a slight curiosity. He was followed in a moment by two more Strangers, going the same way. They were leaving, Eric guessed, before the ceremony began. They probably had ceremonies of their own to attend—with their own people.

Walter the Weapon-Seeker, Arthur the Organizer—were they at this moment sitting in similar storage burrows awaiting the same slow death? Eric doubted it. Somehow he couldn't see these men caught as easily as he and his uncle had been. Arthur was too clever, he was certain of that, and Walter, well, Walter would come up with some fantastic weapon that no one had ever seen or heard of....

Like the one he had in his knapsack right now—that red blob the Weapon-Seeker had given him!

Was it a weapon? He didn't know. But even if it wasn't, he had the impression it could create some kind of surprise. "It should make them sit up and take notice," Walter had said back in Monster territory.

Any kind of surprise, any kind of upset and he might have a diversion under cover of which he and his uncle could escape.

But that was the trouble. His uncle. With his hands bound as thoroughly as he could now ascertain they were, he needed his uncle's help to do anything at all. And the Trap-Smasher was obviously too far gone to be at all useful.

He was talking to himself in a steady, monotonous, argumentative mutter, his upper body slumping further and further across his own lap. Every once in a while, the mutters would be broken by a sharp, almost surprised moan as his wounds woke into a clearer consciousness of themselves.

THE MEN IN THE WALLS

Most other men in his condition, Eric judged, would have been dead by now. Only a body as powerful as the Trap-Smasher's could have lasted this long. And—who knew?—if they could escape, it was possible that his uncle's wounds, given care and rest, might heal.

If they could escape.

      *   *   *   *   *

"Uncle Thomas," he said, leaning toward him and whispering urgently. "I think I know a way out. I think I've figured out a way to escape."

No response. The bloody head continued to talk in a low, toneless voice to the lap. Mutter, mutter, mutter. Moan. Mutter, mutter.

"Your wives," Eric said desperately. "Your wives. Don't you want to get revenge for your wives?"

That seemed to be worth a flicker. "My wives," said the thick voice. "They were good women. Real good women. They never let Franklin near them. They were real good women." Then the flicker was over and the mutters returned.

"Escape!" Eric whispered. "Don't you want to escape?"

A thin, coagulating line of blood dripped out of his uncle's slowly working jaws. There was no other answer.

Eric looked towards the entrance of the storage burrow. The guard posted there was no longer turning from time to time to glance at the prisoners. The structure outside was evidently nearing completion, and his interest in the final preparations had caused him to take a step or two away from the entrance. He was staring off to the left down the great central burrow in absolute fascination.

Well, that was something. It gave them a chance. On the other hand, it also meant that they had scant moments left to their lives. Any time now, the leaders of the Female Society would be coming to drag them to the torture ceremony.

With his eyes on the guard, Eric leaned against the rough burrow wall and began scraping the imprisoning knapsack thongs against the sharpest edges he could find. It wouldn't be fast enough, he realized.

WILLIAM TENN

If there were only a spear point in this place, something sharp. He looked around feverishly. No, nothing. A few tumbled bags of food, over which lazy roaches wandered. Nothing he could use to help him get free.

His uncle was his only hope. Somehow he had to rouse the man, get through to him. He squirmed up close, his mouth against the Trap-Smasher's battered ear.

"This is Eric, Eric the Only. Do you remember me, Uncle? I went on the Theft, Uncle Thomas, I went on the Theft with you. Third category. Remember, I asked for a third category theft, just like you told me to? I did my Theft, I was successful, I made it. I did just what you told me to do. I'm Eric the Eye now, right? Tell me, am I Eric the Eye?"

Mutters, mumbles and moans. The man seemed beyond intelligibility.

"What about Franklin? He can't do this to us, can he, Uncle Thomas? Don't you want to escape? Don't you want revenge on Franklin, on Ottilie, for what they did to your wives? Don't you? *Don't you?*"

He had to cut through his uncle's confused mist of gathering delirium.

In complete desperation, he lowered his head and sank his teeth into a wounded shoulder.

* * * * *

Nothing. Just the steady flow of argumentative gibberish. And the thin blood dripping from the mouth.

"I saw Arthur the Organizer. He said he'd known you for a long time. When did you meet him, Uncle Thomas? When did you first meet Arthur the Organizer?"

The head drooped lower, the shoulders slumped further forward.

"Tell me about Alien-science. What is Alien-science?" Eric was almost gibbering himself now in his frantic efforts to find a key that would unlock his uncle's mind. "Are Arthur the Organizer and

Walter the Weapon-Seeker very important men among the Alien-sciencers? Are they the chiefs? What was the name of the structure they were hiding in? What is it to the Monsters? They talked about other tribes, tribes I never heard of. How many other tribes are there? Are these other tribes—"

That was it. He had found the key. He had gotten through.

Thomas the Trap-Smasher's head came up waveringly, dimness swirling in his eyes. "Other tribes. Funny that you should ask about other tribes. That *you* should ask."

"Why? What about them?" Eric fought to hold the key in place, to keep it turning. "Why shouldn't I ask about those other tribes?"

"Your grandmother was from another tribe, a real strange tribe in a faroff burrow. I remember hearing about it when I was a little boy." Thomas the Trap-Smasher nodded to himself. "Your grandfather's band went on a long journey, the longest they'd ever taken. And they caught your grandmother and brought her back."

    *   *   *   *   *

"My grandmother?" For the moment, Eric forgot what was being prepared for him outside. He'd known there was some peculiar secret about his grandmother. She had rarely been mentioned in Mankind. Up to now, he'd taken it for granted that this was because she'd had a son who was terribly unlucky—almost the worst thing a person in the burrows could be. A one-child litter, after all, and being killed together with his wife in Monster territory. Very unlucky.

"My grandmother was from another tribe? Not from Mankind?" He knew, of course, that several of the women had been captured from other peoples in neighboring burrows and had the good fortune now to be considered full-fledged members of Mankind. Sometimes one of their own women would be lost this way, when she strayed too far down an outlying burrow and stumbled into a band of Stranger warriors. If you stole a woman from another people, after all, you stole a substantial portion of their knowledge. But he'd never imagined—

"Dora the Dream-Singer." Thomas's head waggled loosely: he dribbled words mixed with red saliva. "Did you know why your grandmother was called the Dream-Singer, Eric? The women used to say that the things she talked about happened only in dreams, and that she couldn't talk straight like other people—she could only sing about her dreams. But she taught your father a lot, and he was like her. Women were a little afraid to mate with him. My sister was the first to take a chance—and everyone said she deserved what she got."

Abruptly, Eric became conscious of a change in the sounds outside the burrow. More quiet. Were they coming for him now?

"Uncle Thomas, listen! I have an idea. Those Strangers—Walter, Arthur the Organizer—they gave me a Monster souvenir. I don't know what it does, but I can't get at it. I'll turn around. You try to reach down into my knapsack with the tips of your fingers and—"

The Trap-Smasher paid no attention to him. "She was an Alien-sciencer," he rambled on, mostly to himself. "Your grandmother was the first Alien-sciencer we ever had in Mankind. I guess her tribe were all Alien-sciencers. Imagine—a whole tribe of Alien-sciencers!"

Eric groaned. This half-alive, delirious man was his only hope of escaping. This bloody wreck who had once been the proudest, most alert band captain of them all.

He turned for another look at the guard. The man was still staring down the length of the great central burrow. There was nothing to be heard now but a terrifying silence, as if dozens of pairs of eyes were glowing in anticipation. And footsteps—were not those footsteps? He had to find a way to make his uncle co-operate.

*   *   *   *   *

"Thomas the Trap-Smasher!" he said sharply, barely managing to keep his voice low. "Listen to me. This is an order! There's something in my knapsack, a blob of sticky stuff. We're going to turn our backs to each other, and you're going to reach in with your fingers and fish it out. Do you hear me? That's an order—a warrior's order!"

His uncle nodded, completely docile. "I've been a warrior for over twenty auld lang synes," he mumbled, twisting around. "Six of them a band captain. I've given orders and taken them, given them and taken them. I've never disobeyed an order. What I always say is how can you expect to give orders if you don't—"

"*Now*," Eric told him, bringing their backs together and hunching down so that his knapsack would be just under his uncle's bound arms. "Reach in. Work that mass of sticky stuff out. It's right on top. And hurry!"

Yes. Those were footsteps coming up outside. Several of them. The leaders of the Female Society, the chief, an escort of warriors. And the guard, watching that deadly procession, was liable to remember his duties and turn back to the prisoners.

"*Hurry*," he demanded. "I told you to hurry, dammit! That's an order, too. Get it out fast. Fast!"

And, all this time, as the Trap-Smasher's fumbling fingers wandered about in his knapsack, as he listened with fright and impatience to the sounds of the approaching execution party—all this time, somewhere in his mind, there was wonderment at the orders he was rapping out to an experienced band captain and the incredible authority he had managed to get into his voice.

"Now you're wondering where your grandmother's tribe have their burrow," Thomas began suddenly, reverting to an earlier topic as if they were having a pleasant conversation after a fine, full meal.

"Forget it! Get that stuff out. Just get it out!"

"It's hard to describe," the other man's voice wandered on. "A long way off, their burrow is, a long way off. You know the Strangers call us front-burrow people. You know that, don't you? The Strangers are back-burrowers. Well, your grandmother's people are the bottom-most burrowers of all."

Eric sensed his fingers closing in the knapsack.

The three women who ruled the Female Society came into the storage burrow. Ottilie the Omen-Teller, Sarah the Sickness-Healer and Rita the Record-Keeper. With them was the chief and two band captains, heavily armed.

VIII

Ottilie, the Chieftain's First Wife, was in the lead. She stopped, just inside the entrance to the burrow and the others came to a halt around her.

"Look at them," she jeered. "They're trying to free each other! And what do they plan to do if they get themselves untied?"

Franklin moved to her side and took a long, judicious look at the two men squatting back to back. "They'll try to escape," he explained, continuing his wife's joke. "They'll have their hands free, they figure, and surely Thomas the Trap-Smasher and his nephew are a match, even bare-handed, for the best spearmen in Mankind!"

And then Eric felt the searching hands come up out of the knapsack to which his own arms were tied. Something fell to the floor of the burrow. It made an odd noise, halfway between a splash and a thud. He twisted around for it immediately with his mouth open, flexing his knees in a tight crouch underneath his body.

"You've never seen anything like the burrows of your grandmother's people," his uncle was mumbling, as if what his hands had just done was no concern of the rest of him. "And neither have I, though I've listened to the tales."

"He won't last long now," Sarah the Sickness-Healer commented. "We'll have to have our fun with the boy."

All you do, Walter the Weapon-Seeker had said, *is tear off a pinch with your fingers. Then spit on it and throw it. Throw it as fast and as far as you can.*

He couldn't use his fingers. But he leaned down to the red blob and nipped off a piece with his teeth. He brought his tongue against the strange soft substance, lashing saliva into it. And simultaneously he kicked at the burrow floor with curved toes, straightening his legs, jerking his thighs and body upward. Unable to use his arms for balance, he tottered erect and turned, swaying, to face the leaders of his people.

After you spit on it, throw it fast. As fast and as far as you can.

"I don't know what he's doing," someone said, "but I don't like it. Let me through."

Stephen the Strong-Armed stepped ahead of the group and lifted a heavy spear, ready for throwing.

Eric shut his eyes, bent his head far back on his neck and took a deep, deep breath. Then he snapped his head forward, flipping his tongue hard against the object in his mouth. He forced out his breath so abruptly that the exhalation became a wild, barking cough.

The soft little mass flew out of his mouth, and he opened his eyes to watch its course. For a moment, he was unable to find it anywhere; then he located it by the odd expression on Stephen's face and the fearful upward roll of his eyes.

There was a little red splotch in the middle of the band captain's forehead.

What was supposed to happen, he wondered? He had followed directions as well as he could under the circumstances, but he had no idea what the scarlet stain, made loose and moist by his saliva, was supposed to accomplish. He watched it, hoping and waiting.

Then Stephen the Strong-Armed brought his free hand up slowly to wipe the stuff off. Eric stopped hoping. Nothing was going to happen.

Strangers, he had begun to think despairingly, *that's what comes of trusting Strangers—*

*   *   *   *   *

The blast of sound was so tremendous that for a moment he thought the roof of the burrow had fallen in. He was slammed backwards against the wall and fell as if he'd been walloped with a spear haft. He remembered the cough with which he'd expelled the bit of red blob from his mouth. Had there been a delayed echo to his cough, a gigantic, ear-splitting echo?

He lifted his head from the floor finally, when the reverberations in the little storage burrow had rumbled into a comparative silence. Someone was screaming. Someone was screaming over and over again.

It was Sarah. She was looking at Stephen the Strong-Armed from the rear. She had been standing directly behind him. Now she was staring at him and screaming in sharp steady bursts.

Her mouth was open so wide that it seemed she was about to tear her jaws apart. And with each scream she lifted her arm rigidly and pointed to the back of Stephen's neck. She kept lifting her arm and pointing as if she wanted everyone present to know beyond the least doubt why and how she came to be screaming.

Stephen the Strong-Armed had no head. His body ended at the neck, and flaps of skin fell down to his chest in an irregular wavy pattern. A fountain of blood bubbled and spurted where his head had been. His body still stood upright, feet planted wide apart in a good warrior's stance, one arm holding the spear ready for action and the other congealed in its upward motion to wipe the red blob away. It stood, incredibly straight and tall and alive.

Suddenly, it fell apart.

First the spear slid slowly forward out of the right hand and clattered to the floor. Then the arms began to fall loosely to the sagging knees and the entire great, brawny body slumped as if its bones had left it. It dropped aimlessly to the floor, an arm poking out here, a leg twisting out there, in a pattern as meaningless as if an oddly shaped bag of skin had been flung to one side of the burrow.

It continued to twitch for a moment or two, as the bubbling fountain of blood turned into a sluggishly flowing river. At last it lay still, a motionless heap of limbs and torso. Of the missing head there was no trace anywhere.

*　　　*　　　*　　　*　　　*

THE MEN IN THE WALLS

Sarah the Sickness-Healer stopped screaming and turned, shaking, to her companions. Their protruding eyes left the body on the floor.

Then they all reacted at once.

They yelled madly, wildly, fearfully, as if they were a chorus and she the conductor. Still bellowing, they made for the narrow entrance behind them. They got through in a pushing, punching scramble that at one point looked like a composite monster with dozens of arms, legs and swinging, naked breasts. They carried the guard outside with them, and with them, too, they carried their uncontrollable panic, screaming it into existence all along the great central burrow.

For a little while, Eric could hear feet pounding into the distant corridors. Then there was quiet. There was quiet everywhere, except for Thomas the Trap-Smasher's interminable mumbling.

Eric forced himself upright again. He was unable to imagine what had happened. That red blob—the Stranger, Walter, had said it was a weapon, but it didn't operate like any weapon he had ever in his life heard of. Except possibly in the times of the ancestors: the ancestors were supposed to have had things which could blow an object apart and leave no trace. But this was an alien artifact, a possession of the Monsters which Walter the Weapon-Seeker had somehow found and appropriated. What was it? How had it exploded the head of Stephen the Strong-Armed?

That was to be worked out another time. Meanwhile, he had his chance. It might not last long: he had no idea when the panic might subside and a patrol of warriors be sent back to investigate. He stepped carefully across the red stream flowing from the fallen man's neck. Squatting down in front of the dropped spear, he managed to get a grip on it with his bound hands and rose, holding it awkwardly behind him.

No time to cut his bonds. Not here.

"Uncle Thomas," he called. "We can get away. We have a chance now. Come on, get up!"

The wounded band captain stared up at him without comprehension. "—corridors like you've never seen or imagined," he continued in a low monotone. "Glow lamps that aren't on foreheads. Corridors filled with glow lamps. Corridors and corridors and corridors—"

For a moment, Eric considered. The man would be a heavy liability in fast travel. But he couldn't desert him. This was his last surviving relative, the only person who didn't consider him an outlaw and a thing. And, shattered as he was, also still his captain.

"Get up!" he said again. "Thomas the Trap-Smasher, get up! That's an order, a warrior's order. Get up!"

As he'd hoped, his uncle responded to the old command. He managed to get his legs under his body, and strained against them, but it was no use. He didn't have the energy to rise.

* * * * *

Casting apprehensive looks over his shoulder at the entrance to the storage burrow, Eric ran to the struggling man. Working backwards, he managed to get one end of the spear under the crook of his uncle's arm. Then, using his own hip as a fulcrum, he levered hard at the other end.

It was painful, slippery work, since he couldn't bring all of his muscles into play and it was difficult to see what he was doing. In between efforts, he gasped out orders to "Get up, get up, get *up*, damn you!" At last the end of the spear went all the way down. His uncle was on his feet, staggering, but at least on his feet.

Dragging the spear awkwardly, Eric urged and butted him out of the place. The great central burrow was empty of people. Weapons, pots and miscellaneous possessions lay strewn about where they had been dropped. The finished structure of the Stage stood deserted in front of the royal mound. And some time before, the bodies of his uncle's wives had evidently been removed.

The chief and the other leaders had bolted to the left once they had clawed their way out of the storage burrow. They had apparently run past the scaffold structure and picked up the rest of Mankind in their panic.

Eric turned right.

His uncle was a problem. Thomas the Trap-Smasher kept coming to a bewildered halt. Again and again he began the story of his long-ago journey to the burrows of the strange, distant tribe. Eric had to push against him to keep him moving.

Once they were in the outlying corridors, he felt better. But not until they had made many turns, passed dozens of branches and were well into completely uninhabited burrows, did he feel he could stop and saw himself free of his bonds on the point of the spear. He did the same for his uncle. Then, throwing the Trap-Smasher's left arm across his own shoulders and clutching him tightly about the waist, he started off again. It was slow going: his uncle was a heavy man, but the more distance they could put between themselves and Mankind, the better.

But distance where? Where should they go? He pondered the problem as they tottered together down the silent, branching corridors. One place was as good as another. There was nowhere that they would be welcome. Just keep going.

He may have muttered his questions aloud. To his surprise, Thomas the Trap-Smasher suddenly said in an entirely coherent but very weak voice: "The doorway to Monster territory, Eric. Make for the doorway to Monster territory where you went to make your Theft."

"Why?" Eric asked. "What can we do there?"

There was no answer. His uncle's head fell forward on his chest. He was evidently sliding into a stupor again. And yet, somehow, as long as Eric's encircling arm pulled at his body, the man's legs kept moving forward. There was some residual stamina and a warrior's determination in him yet.

Monster territory. Was there more safety for them there now than they could find among human beings?

Very well then. The doorway to Monster territory. They would have to come around in a wide arc through many corridors to get to it, but Eric knew the way. He was Eric the Eye, after all, he told himself: it was his business always to know the way.

But was it? He had not enjoyed the formal initiation into manhood that was the usual aftermath of a successful Theft. Without that, perhaps he was still Eric the Only, still a boy and an initiate. No, he knew what he was. He was Eric the Outlaw, nothing else.

He was an outlaw, without a home and a people. And, except for the dying man he pulled along, everyone's hand was henceforth against him.

IX

Thomas the Trap-Smasher had been badly injured in the surprise attack that had wiped out his band. Ordinarily, he would have had his wounds carefully dressed by the cleverness and accumulated experience of Sarah the Sickness-Healer. Under the circumstances, however, Sarah had done the reverse.

Now, the strain of escape and the forced headlong flight that followed it had emptied his body of its last resources. His eyes were glazed and his strong shoulders hung slack. He was a somnambulist walking jerkily in the direction of death.

When they stopped to rest, Eric—after listening intently for any sounds of pursuit—had washed his uncle's wounds carefully with water from the canteens and had bound the uglier gashes with strips torn from a knapsack. It was all he knew how to do: warrior's first aid. A woman's advanced therapeutic knowledge was needed for anything more complicated.

Not that it would have made very much difference by this time. The Trap-Smasher was too far gone.

Eric felt desperate at the thought of being left alone forever in the dark, uninhabited corridors. He tried to force water and bits of food upon his uncle. The man's head rolled back, nourishment dribbling carelessly down from both sides of his mouth. He was breathing lightly and very rapidly. His body had grown quite warm by the time they stopped.

Eric himself ate ravenously: it was his first meal in a long, long while. He kept staring at his recumbent uncle and trying to work out a line of action that would do some good. In the end, he had thought of nothing better than to hitch the man's arm up over his shoulder again and to keep going in the direction of Monster territory.

Once erect, the Trap-Smasher's feet began walking again, but with a dragging, soggy quality that became more and more pronounced. After a while, Eric had to come to a halt: he had the feeling that he was hauling dead weight.

When he tried to lower his uncle to the floor of the burrow, he found that the body had become almost completely limp. Thomas lay on his back, his eyes staring without curiosity at the rounded ceiling upon which his forehead glow-lamp outlined a bright circular patch.

The heartbeat was very, very faint.

"Eric," he heard a weak voice say. He raised his eyes from his uncle's chest and looked at the painfully working mouth.

"Yes, uncle?"

"I'm sorry—about—what I got you into. I had—no right. Your life—after all—your life. You—my wives—the band. I led—death—everyone. I'm sorry."

Eric fought hard to hold back his tears. "It was for a reason, Uncle Thomas," he said. "We had a cause. It wasn't just you. The cause failed."

There was a hideous cackle from the prone man. For a moment, Eric thought it was a death rattle. Then he realized that it had been a laugh, but such a laugh as he had never heard before.

"A cause?" the Trap-Smasher gasped. "A cause? Do you know—do you—know what—the cause was? I wanted—wanted to be chief. Chief. The only—only way I could—do it—Alien-science—the

Strangers—a cause. Everyone—the killings—I wanted to—to be chief. *Chief!*"

He went rigid as he coughed out the last word. Then slowly, like flesh turning into liquid, he relaxed.

He was dead.

*   *   *   *   *

Eric stared at the body a long time. It didn't make any difference, he found. The numbness in his mind remained. There was a great paralyzed spot in the center of his brain that was unable to think or to feel.

In the end, he shook himself, bent down and grabbed the body by the shoulders. Walking backwards, he dragged it in the direction of Monster territory.

Something he had to do. The duty of anyone who lived in the burrows when death occurred in his neighborhood. Now it filled time and used up energies that he might otherwise have expended in thoughts which were agonizing.

The energies which it demanded were almost more than he was capable of at this point. His uncle had been a heavy, well built man. Eric found that he had to stop at the end of almost every curving corridor and get his breath back.

He finally arrived at the doorway, grateful for the fact that his uncle had died so relatively close to it. He also felt he understood why this had been suggested as their destination. Thomas the Trap-Smasher had known he had little time left. His nephew would have the responsibility of sewering him. He had tried to make it as easy for Eric as possible by going the greater part of the distance on his own feet.

There was a fresh-water pipe in the wall near the doorway to Monster territory. And wherever there was a fresh-water pipe, the Monsters were likely to have laid a sewer pipe nearby. It was down this, probably, that the men killed in the battle with Stephen the Strong-Armed's band had been disposed of much earlier. And it was down this that Thomas had known his remains must also go—the closest point at which his nephew could sewer him in comparative safety.

This much, at least, he had done for Eric's benefit.

Eric located the fresh-water pipe without much difficulty. There was a constant low rumbling and gurgling underfoot, and—at the spot where it was most pronounced—he found the slab in the floor cut at the cost of infinite labor by some past generation of Mankind. Near it, after the slab was lifted, was another, much thicker pipe, large enough to carry two men abreast. Like the other one, the hard stuff of the burrow floor had been scraped away so that a joint lay exposed.

Opening the joint was another matter. Eric had seen it done many times by his elders, but this was his own first attempt. It was a tricky business of tugging a heavy covering plate first right, then left, and getting his fingers under the rim and pulling at just the right moment.

*   *   *   *   *

The joint opened at last, and the incredible stink of Monster sewage poured out as the liquid swirled darkly by. Death had always been associated in Eric's mind with this stink, since the pipe carried not only the Monster's waste matter but also that of Mankind, collected from its burrows every week by the old women who were too feeble for any other work. All that was not alive or useful was carried to the nearest Monster sewer pipe, all that might decay and foul the burrows. And that included, of course, the bodies of the dead.

Eric stripped his uncle's body of all useful gear as he had seen the women do many times. Then he dragged it to the hole in the burrow floor and held it by one arm for a moment as the current of the sewage caught it. He repeated as much of the ceremony as he could remember, concluding with the words: *"And therefore, O ancestors, I beg you to receive the body of this member of Mankind, Thomas the*

Trap-Smasher, a warrior of the first rank, a band captain of renown and the father of nine."

There was usually another line or so—"*Take him to you and keep him with you until the time when the Monsters have been destroyed utterly and the Earth is ours again. Then shall you and he and all human beings who have ever lived rise from the sewers and joyously walk the surface of our world forever.*" But this, after all, was a pure Ancestor-science passage; and his uncle had died fighting Ancestor-science. What was the Alien-science equivalent? Was it likely to be any more potent, any less full of falsehood? In the end, Eric omitted those last two lines.

He let go of the stiffening arm. The body shot away and down the pipe. Thomas the Trap-Smasher was gone, he was gone for all time, the way Eric reasoned now. He was dead and sewered, and that was that.

Eric closed the joint, pulled the slab down and stamped it into place.

He was completely alone. An outlaw who could expect nothing from other human beings but death by slow torture. He had no companions, no home, no beliefs of any sort. His uncle's last words still lay, in all their stern ugliness, at the bottom of his mind. "*I wanted to—to be chief.*"

*   *   *   *   *

It was bad enough to discover that the religion on which he had been raised was a mere prop to the power of the chieftainship, that the mysterious Female Society was completely unable to see into a person's future. But to find out that his uncle's thoughtful antagonism to such nonsense was based on nothing more substantial than simple personal ambition, an ambition murderously unscrupulous and willing to sacrifice anybody who trusted him—well, what was there left to believe in, to base a life upon?

Had his father and mother been any less gullible than the most naive child in the burrows? They had sacrificed themselves—for what? For one superstition as opposed to another, for the secret political maneuvers of this person as opposed to that.

Not for him. He would be free. He laughed, bitterly and self-consciously. He had to be free. There was no choice: he was an outlaw.

Eric walked a few steps and put his hands on the door to Monster territory. To shift it out of its socket was a hard job for one man. He strained and tore his fingers; finally he managed it. The door came away and he deposited it carefully on the floor of the burrow.

He stared at it for a while, trying to figure out a way of getting it back after he'd passed through the doorway. No, a single man just couldn't do that from the other side. He'd have to leave the doorway open, an incredible social crime.

Well, he couldn't commit a crime any more. He was beyond all rules made by human communities. Ahead lay the glaring white light that he and his kind feared so much. Into this he would go. Here, where there were no illusions to be found and no help to be expected, here he would make his solitary outlaw home.

Behind him lay the dark, safe, intricate burrows. They were tunnels, Eric knew now, in the walls that surrounded Monster territory. Men lived in these walls, and shivered, and were ignorant, and made fools of each other. He could no longer do these things: he had to face the Monsters. He wanted to face them and destroy them.

It was like one of the roaches in the storage burrow declaring war on a cook who came in to make the evening meal for Mankind. The cook would roar with laughter at such a thought. Who knew what went on in the mind of a roach—and who cared? Yet the roach would enjoy two special advantages. He had once and for all stopped crawling greedily and aimlessly with his own kind; and the enemy he had selected could regard him with nothing more than heavy oblivious contempt. If he could ever for a moment find one usable weapon and one vital area on which that weapon could be used....

WILLIAM TENN

He hefted his two special advantages grimly. Then Eric the Only, the Eye, the Outlaw, Eric the Self-Aware Individual Man, stepped through the doorway into Monster territory.

www.ingramcontent.com/pod-product-compliance
Lightning Source LLC
Chambersburg PA
CBHW030539180626
46810CB00005B/1929